The Rainmakers

About the author

Paul Kisakye is a Ugandan-born writer, editor and writing coach. He is the author of the *Tech Explorers League*, a series of sci-fi novels for children; and a non-fiction book *Prodigal Love*. He is an African Writers Trust Publishing Fellow and was shortlisted for the Writivism Short Story Prize in 2013 for his piece, "Emotional Roller Coaster".

The Rainmakers

Paul Kisakye

Amalion
BP 5637 Dakar-Fann
Dakar CP 10700
Senegal
http://www.amalion.net

ISBN 978-2-35926-102-8 (paperback)
ISBN 978-2-35926-103-5 (ebook)

Cover designed by Anke Rosenlocher

This publication was produced under the Culture at Work Africa Programme implemented by the Arts & Culture programme at Université Abdou Moumouni, Niger in partnership with Amalion, with the financial support of the European Union. Its contents are the sole responsibility of the author and do not necessarily reflect the views of the European Union.

To Crispus, my dearest brother

1

I sit up in bed and stretch my arms. The morning sunlight is already streaming through my bedroom window.

"Oh no! Not again!" I say to myself at the thought of another day of video games at Uncle James's house.

Pulling back the duvet over my head, I try to get some more sleep. But I have used up all my sleep. I never sleep this long during the school term. I'm always up by six and out of the house by six thirty, just in time to catch the school bus to Mukungu High School. When the term ended, I was looking forward to sleeping through the morning. But now even sleep has become boring.

Frustrated, I get out of bed and trudge to the bathroom for a shower.

After the shower, I go downstairs and find Mum has already left for work. Thanks to waking up late, I no longer see her in the mornings. Dad is seated in his favourite armchair, reading a book.

"Good morning, Dad."

"Tendo! I see you still haven't got tired of waking up late," Dad says, looking up from his book, his half-moon-shaped wire-rimmed reading glasses halfway down the bridge of his nose. "You'll become lazy."

"No more waking up late for me," I reply. "I feel like I've done all the sleeping there is to do for the rest of the holiday."

"Good! So, what are you doing today?"

I touch my chin, trying to think up something fun to do today. "Same thing I did yesterday."

"Oh. What was that?"

"Same thing I did the day before."

Dad nods his head. He is forgetful and I enjoy teasing him about it.

"Your uncle Moses is coming to visit us today," Dad says. "I'm going to pick him up at the airport this afternoon."

"Uncle Moses is coming to visit us?" I ask, surprised. I've heard a little about Dad's older brother from stories Dad has told me, but I'm yet to meet him.

"Yes. And he'll be staying for Christmas."

"That's so cool!" I say. Living in a large four-bedroom house with only my parents can get lonely at times. Sometimes I wish I wasn't an only child with no other relatives living close by. Today, I'll finally get to meet Dad's brother. I hope he is as cool as my dad.

"I'll need you to be on your best behaviour while he's here," Dad says.

"Sure."

It's not like I'm not always on my best behaviour. Apart from hacking my way around parental controls on my phone and tab so I can watch some videos a fifteen-year-old boy shouldn't watch—according to my parents—I am a pretty decent guy.

I saunter to the kitchen and get out a bowl from a cupboard. I pour some Choco Pops in it, open the fridge, get out cold milk and drown the Choco Pops in it. With a tablespoon, I stuff the cereal down my throat. Ten minutes later, I'm out of the house, on my way to Uncle James's house.

****

Dr James Mugonyi, an award-winning scientist and inventor, is Dad's closest friend. He is the uncle I have never met. I've known him for as long as I can remember. His twin son and daughter, Kato and Babirye, are my closest and oldest friends. When we were little, Mum or Dad would ferry me to Uncle James's house for play dates with the twins since we were age-mates. I am only three months older than them.

Uncle James's house is on a street lined with identical houses built by the same real estate company. My friends and I love hanging out at his house because he has the best video game console ever. And he is not as strict as my dad about how long we play video games.

As soon as I ring the doorbell, the door flies open and Atlas, Uncle James's Virtual Assistant, speaks through speakers hidden in the wall.

"Tendo," Atlas says in a smooth, female voice, "you're late. Overslept again?"

"It's the holidays, Atlas," I say, entering the house. The door slowly closes behind me. "It's the only time I get to sleep till I can sleep no more."

"Your friends have been waiting for you for forty-eight minutes now in the basement."

I head straight to the basement, which has what Uncle James calls his man cave, an entertainment centre that has high-tech gadgets that are straight out of a science fiction movie.

"Hey guys!" I say.

Kunda, a short guy who always acts younger than his age, even though he is the oldest of us all, is playing a car racing game with Kato, a tall, lean guy with an athletic build. Babirye, who also happens to be the most beautiful girl I've ever seen, sits on a stool, arms crossed on her chest, pouting.

"I can't play alone with these guys," Babirye says. "They are better than me. Where have you been, Tendo?"

"In my bed," I say. "Where else would I be?"

"So, are you also going to join them?" Babirye asks me.

Growing up, she was almost identical to her brother, but in the last two years, she has changed into a young woman. The angles on her body have softened into pleasant curves. Although she is still a tomboy, and still loves wearing her brother's shorts and tee-shirts, she has lost her boyish looks. Long, thick eyelashes frame her big brown eyes. Her thick, curly hair is tamed into a ponytail.

I blink and remind myself to stop staring. I've been doing that a lot lately, having to remind myself to stop staring at Babirye. Although I've watched her transformation from girl to woman over the years—her and Kato are like the siblings I never had—I can't help but be mesmerised by her beauty now.

2

"I'm not playing anymore," I announce.

Kunda and Kato pause their game.

"Why?" Kato asks, his brow raised in surprise.

Kunda, his hands still gripping the video game control like his life depends on it, says, "Because we keep beating you at it?"

For as long as I can remember, when playing video games, Kunda always teams up with Kato and Babirye teams up with me. Babirye and I get beaten more often than we care to count.

"I'm tired of playing," I say. "We need to come up with other things to do."

"But we're having fun," Kato says.

Babirye, turning to Kato, says, "Not all of us are having fun!"

"She has a point," I tell Kato.

Kato puts down the video game control and slumps into a bean bag. Removing his black-framed glasses, he cleans them with the hem of his tee-shirt. "What do you suggest we do?" he asks Babirye.

"We could go upstairs and watch a movie," comes a voice from a dark corner of the basement.

"No way I'm watching another chick flick," Kunda says, crossing his arms on his ample belly.

"Sanyu?" I say, squinting to make out the dark form huddled in another bean bag in the darkness.

"Hi Tendo," Sanyu, the only other girl in our group says. She has a small, round face and her hair is braided into neat cornrows. Babirye introduced her to our group last holiday, partly because she didn't want to be the only girl in the group, and partly because Sanyu, being the newest girl in our class—her family moved from Kampala three months ago—didn't have any other friends at school.

"Why are you hiding in the corner?" I ask Sanyu.

"Since you guys have never let me play video games with you, I thought I could as well go ahead and hibernate."

'Hibernate' is Sanyu's buzzword for day-dreaming. She does that a lot, goes into her head and starts thinking up crazy theories in physics. No wonder she's the smartest girl in our class. She topped our class last term, even though it was her first term. Now everyone in our class is wondering if our school is up to the same academic standard as the schools in the capital city, where Sanyu came from.

"You could play in my place," I say under my breath, embarrassed. But no one hears me.

When Sanyu joined us, she destabilised the balance in our tight-knit group. First of all, it was now hard to add her to any team. The Kato-Kunda team—although they were better at video games than the Tendo-Babirye team—wouldn't let Sanyu join us, because they said it would be unfair.

To make matters worse, Kato had started dating Sanyu. We were all acting like it was the most normal thing in the world, but I knew that all of us found it weird seeing the two lovebirds with their hands all over each other whenever we were hanging out. Babirye had finally got a best friend who was a girl for the first time in her life, and her brother had gone ahead and made moves on her friend. She called it puppy love and kept hinting that it wouldn't last.

"See?" Babirye says, suddenly standing up and getting animated. "Even Sanyu finds video games boring!"

"That's because she isn't playing. And it wouldn't be fair to any team if she joined the other team," Kunda adds.

Kunda, the ever insensitive one with virtually no emotional intelligence. But I can't say that out loud, lest it causes more instability in our group.

"Then I'm also suggesting that we go find something to do that we'll all enjoy," Sanyu says. She walks over to where we are so she can join in on the conversation.

"That's three to two," I say. "If we are to be democratic, then we should stop playing video games."

"But we'll be bored," Kato complains.

"We're already bored," his sister quips.

"So, apart from watching chick flicks," Kunda says, "what do you suggest we should do?"

"Personally, I'd love to learn how to farm with my hands," Sanyu says. "Of course, I know how to do it theoretically, and I know no one really does farming with their hands any more. But I'd love to try and grow something living on my own."

"And how do you think you are going to do that?" Kato asks. He doesn't seem convinced that we all need to take a break from playing video games.

"We could go to Tendo's father's farm. I'm sure he has seeds we can use. I think it will be adventurous."

"I hate farming," Kunda declares.

"Have you ever done it before?" I ask.

"No, but it involves getting your hands dirty."

"I'll get you gloves," I say.

"I love the idea. Let's do it!" says Babirye excitedly.

3

The man cave door opens and Uncle James enters. He is a tall, lanky old man with thick black-rimmed glasses. His face is like Kato's face put in an aging app, glasses and all. He is always dressed in a black tee-shirt, blue jeans and black Oxford shoes. I once asked him why he's always practically in the same clothes and he said that he has to make so many decisions every day, and he didn't want what to wear to be one of them.

"No video games this morning?" he asks us.

"Some people are tired of playing," Kato says.

With a cheery voice, Sanyu adds, "We are going farming!"

"I think that will be much more fun than video games," Uncle James says. "You are going to Tendo's father's farm to do this farming, right?"

"Yes," I say. "That's where we are going now."

"I'm dropping off a few things at Makanika's repair shop. I could give you guys a lift up to the repair shop if you don't mind."

"Thank you, Uncle James." I say.

Uncle James walks to his storage units at the far end of the man cave, opens one and gets out four boxes, one by one, placing them on a table. Each box is about the size of my bedside table.

"Dad, can we help you carry these to the car?" Kato asks.

"Sure. Thank you," Uncle James says.

I pick up one box. Kunda and Kato pick up the other two. Babirye is going to pick up the fourth one but Sanyu beats her to it.

"Whoa! This is heavy!" Kunda says. "What's inside, Uncle James?"

Uncle James leads the way to the front of the house where his minivan is waiting. "Rainmakers," he says.

"Rainmakers?" says Babirye. "They make rain?"

"Something like that. They don't actually manufacture rain. They use something called omicron rays to move clouds from a place where it's going to rain to the place where you want it to rain."

"That's awesome!" I say. "So why are you taking them to Mr Makanika's repair shop?"

"I can't use them," Uncle James says. "I failed to get a government licence to use them. They said that competing farmers could use them to destroy their competitors' farms by redirecting rain from the competitors' farms. That would give an unfair advantage to whoever can afford them."

We load the Rainmakers into the boot of the car.

"Shotgun!" Kato calls out and runs to the passenger side of the minivan.

His sister shakes her head. "Boys!" she mutters.

Uncle James gets into the driver's seat. The rest of us board too and we drive off to Mr Makanika's repair shop.

"Dad?" Babirye says as Uncle James joins Main Street. "What if a place hasn't had rain for a long time and they badly need it? Wouldn't the Rainmakers help them?"

"That's what I told the government," Uncle James replies. "They said that irrigation has been working well so far.

They don't see why people shouldn't use that instead of the Rainmakers."

"What's irrigation?" Kato asks.

"Dude, you don't know irrigation?" I say. "That's why you need to learn some farming."

Babirye, turning to her brother in the front passenger seat, says, "Irrigation is simply the watering of crops through a system that moves water from one place to another, you dummy." Then, going back to the previous topic, she adds, "I think the government is just afraid that the Rainmakers' technology is disruptive."

"You are a smart girl, Babirye," Uncle James says.

Babirye beams. There is a twinkle in her big brown eyes.

And I don't know why my heart skips a beat.

We get to Mr Makanika's repair shop, a large warehouse where you can have anything electronic fixed, or buy it second-hand. The repair shop gate opens automatically and Uncle James drives in.

The repair shop has large, metallic industrial shelves filled with second-hand home and industrial appliances and spare parts.

"Dr James!" Mr Makanika shouts from his office in the corner of the warehouse. "I had a feeling that would be you! How are you?"

Mr Makanika, a thickset middle-aged man with a permanent scowl on his face, stands at the entrance to his office. He is dressed in dark blue work overalls with his name, Musa, stencilled on his left breast. I've never heard anyone refer to him as Musa though.

Kunda, Kato and I pick up the boxes of Rainmakers from the boot of the car. Uncle James gets the last one and he leads us to Mr Makanika's office.

Mr Makanika's attention is taken by the boxes we are carrying. "What have you got for me today?" he asks.

"Rainmakers," Kunda says.

"What in the world are those?"

"They make rain but Dad can't use them," Babirye says.

Mr Makanika asks why and she tells him.

"Hmmm…" Mr Makanika says, scratching his scraggly grey beard. "Does that mean I can't put them online and sell them the way they are?"

"No, you can't," Uncle James says. "But you can sell their parts. Half of the materials I used to build them came from your shop. That's why I've brought them to you."

4

Mukungu is a town in north-eastern Uganda. The town has one main street, which makes it easy to navigate without the need for Google Maps. Main Street divides the town into two. The northern side is an estate of identical double-storeyed houses, all built by the same company, housing the wealthier members of the community. That's where Kato and Babirye live. The southern side has Mukungu Primary School, Mukungu High School, Mukungu Stadium, and two farming estates, one of them owned by my dad.

Due to the advent of big supermarket chains, with one located on the outskirts of the town and closer to other bigger towns, most of the shops lining both sides of Main Street in the town were turned into apartments. This is where Kunda and Sanyu live: Kunda with his lawyer mother, who hires a babysitter for him whenever she travels for business, which is almost all the time; and Sanyu with her retrenched father, writer mother and three younger brothers in a two-bedroom apartment.

"Grab yourselves a scooter and let's go out for a ride," I tell my friends.

We have walked from Mr Makanika's repair shop to my home and are now in Dad's workshop, a warehouse behind the main house on our estate. This is where Dad does most of his work and stores the farm equipment. It's like his farm's control centre.

My father's farm is so large—six hundred acres, according to some official documents I've seen—that he needs drones to supervise the work he is doing on it. If his physical presence is needed in any part of the vast farmland, there are a few small and light electric quad scooters that he uses to get around. Every now and then, he receives clients, fellow farmers or government officials coming to tour his farm. These quad scooters come in handy on such days.

Today, they will come in handy. Before we try out some farming, we are going to take a ride around the farm. Dad would never let me ride one of these scooters without him around to supervise and make sure that I don't get hurt. He forgets that I am now old enough to take good care of myself.

Dad has gone to pick Uncle Moses from the airport and Mum is away at work. That means we have the whole estate to ourselves, and can do as we please.

"I thought we are here to farm," Sanyu says.

"That's right," I say. "But first, we'll have some fun."

"Does that mean farming isn't fun?"

"I didn't say that."

"But it's what you meant."

"Okay," I say, exasperated. Sometimes I feel like telling Sanyu off for being such a smarty-pants. "We're going to do some farming, which is actually lots of fun. But first, we'll take these scooters for a ride. I think it will also be lots of fun. So, everyone, to your scooters!"

"I don't think I can ride," Sanyu says.

"Don't be silly," Babirye tells her.

"But I've never ridden one," Sanyu says, her brow etched with concern, "and I last rode a bicycle like five years ago."

"You are the smartest girl I've ever seen. I'm sure it won't be that hard for you."

"Well, if you say so."

Sanyu gingerly straddles a scooter and sits on its seat.

The rest of us also get onto our scooters and start them.

"Whoa!" Sanyu exclaims as her scooter vibrates as soon as she starts it.

Then she shoots out of the workshop door, screaming.

We burst out into laughter at her.

"Let's go after her before she hurts herself or causes damage to anything," I say.

I lead the way and we head out into the farm.

Sanyu, having failed to control her scooter, has ended up leaving havoc in her wake. Wherever she's gone, she has left maize stalks bent out of her way.

"Oh no!" I say. "This isn't cool at all!"

Baaaang!

The crashing sound in the distance makes me flinch.

"Sanyu!" I shout.

No reply.

5

"Sanyu must be hurt!" Babirye says. "Let's go find her."

We ride our scooters in a single file through the destroyed maize stalks, taking the same path that Sanyu has taken.

"Sanyu?" I call out again.

Still, Sanyu doesn't answer.

What has happened to Sanyu? I am starting to get scared, fearing for the worst. This had been my idea. And now Sanyu could have crashed into something and got herself hurt.

"Sanyu?" Babirye calls out. There's a tremor in her voice.

My mind is racing, imagining all sorts of terrible things we are going to find at the end of the destroyed maize plants.

After about three minutes of riding our scooters at breakneck speed, we finally find her.

She is lying on the ground, part of the scooter on top of her, idling. Some maize stalks have fallen over them.

"Sanyu?" Babirye whispers, going down on her knees and gingerly touching Sanyu's head. "Noooooo!" she cries out.

Kunda, Kato and I also get off our scooters and move closer. Kunda and Kato lift the scooter off Sanyu. She is lying still, not moving. Her pink tee-shirt and jeans are now dirty and there is a smudge of soil on her left cheek.

This doesn't look good.

Lying a few metres away is a plant pod. The small cylinder has a small crack and a greenish fluid is oozing out. That's what Sanyu crashed into.

Babirye is frozen, eyes as wide as saucers, her jaw almost dropping to the ground.

Kato crouches down and puts his arm around her. "It's okay. She's going to be fine," he whispers in her ear.

Then he sits on the ground, lifts Sanyu's head and puts it on his lap. With his thumb, he wipes the smudge of soil on her cheek.

Kunda just stands astride his scooter and stares, his hands clasped in front of his belly.

I put two fingers on Sanyu's neck, feeling for the carotid artery. Her heart is beating steadily, pumping blood to her head. I'm surprised at the calmness that washes over me.

"Is she dead?" Babirye whispers.

"No," I say. The impact of the fall must have knocked her out. I gently shake her shoulders and say, "Sanyu. Sanyu. Wake up!"

Sanyu's eyelids flutter and she opens her eyes. "What just happened?" she says, her voice a croaky whisper.

Babirye screams, pushes Kato away, and wraps Sanyu in a tight embrace.

Sanyu slowly lifts her arms and puts them around the hysterical girl. "Careful, Babirye," Sanyu says. "I think I bruised a rib or something. Damn! My head hurts!"

Babirye, both hands on Sanyu's shoulder, looks the girl over, her brow furrowed. "Sanyu, are you okay? You just fainted!"

"I'm fine," Sanyu says, smiling. "Just a little dizzy, but that will pass too with some rest."

No one seems convinced.

"I'm okay. Sanyu says. "I swear, guys. No need to worry."

"I'm your boyfriend. Of course I worry."

Sanyu sighs and rolls her eyes. "Look guys, I am fine. Probably need to go home early."

"You are sure you don't need to go to the hospital and get checked out?" Kato asks.

"Cut it out, Kato!" Sanyu raises her voice. I've never heard her raise her voice before. "You have only known me a couple of months and now you think you know all about me? If I say I'm okay, I'm okay. I already have my parents to worry about me. I won't have my friends do that too. Now, can we forget this happened and go on with our lives?"

No one says a word for a few moments. Kunda is still standing astride his scooter, his hands clasped on his belly, but now his mouth is also open. Kato's jaws are set and moving. I think he is grinding his teeth and forcing his mouth to remain shut so he doesn't say what is on his mind. Babirye's brow is still furrowed, but I can't imagine what's going on in her mind.

Finally, I break the silence and say, "Sanyu, can you get up and try walking?"

Sanyu tries to hoist herself up with her arms, but fails. "Give me a hand, guys," she says.

Kato and I put our hands under Sanyu's armpits and pull her up. Sanyu stumbles a bit but finally gains her footing.

"See?" she says, raising her arms and awkwardly twirling, a plastic smile on her face, "I'm perfectly fine."

"We have a problem," I say. "The house is too far away for you to walk back. Can you use the scooter?"

"Good idea, Tendo," Sanyu says. "What would you like me to crash into this time? Just point at it."

We all laugh. The accident is soon forgotten.

"I'm sorry, guys," Sanyu says, "but I'm not getting on a scooter any time soon. You go right ahead. I'll find you."

Kato says, "Just hop onto my scooter. As long as you can hold tightly onto me, we'll reach the workshop safely."

"Thank you, Kato," Sanyu says and lifts herself carefully onto Kato's scooter.

I fasten Sanyu's scooter onto the back of my scooter.

Then we ride back to the house.

After we have put away the scooters in the workshop, and cleaned off as much dirt as we can from our clothes, we walk to the main house.

Roaring laughter comes from the house.

"Where is my favourite nephew in the whole world?" comes a deep, loud voice.

Uncle Moses is home.

6

"John! You told me I had only one nephew!"

My friends and I are standing in front of a gigantic man who seems to be inspecting us. Uncle Moses has a silly grin on his face.

"That's right, Moses," Dad says. His head is buried in the fridge as he rummages through it for something to drink. "That's your nephew Tendo and his friends."

Uncle Moses says, "Looks like you guys have been up to some mischief on the farm, judging by the dirt on your clothes, huh? So, which one of you is Tendo?"

I lift up one hand like I'm in class offering to give an answer to a question the teacher has asked. Uncle Moses takes one step forward and crushes my ribs in one heck of a bear hug. I can feel his rock-hard torso muscles through the tight white tee-shirt he is wearing.

"Look how big you've grown!" he says in a booming voice that threatens to burst my eardrums. He holds me at arm's length, inspects me, and continues, "Last time I saw you, you were a tiny little baby of less than one year. Do you remember me?"

I shake my head. There's no way I can remember anything about this guy. From the corner of my eye, I can see Babirye rolling her eyes.

"Come on now, introduce me to your friends," Uncle Moses says.

Dad hands Uncle Moses a can of energy drink, the kind I'm not allowed to drink. Dad also rarely drinks them. He sometimes has to throw out the expired cans. It's only Mum who sometimes drinks them when she has to work throughout the night. "There!" he says to Uncle Moses. "I know how you love your energy drinks."

Uncle Moses cracks the lid open with large, beefy hands, takes a swig of the ice-cold drink, then smacks his lips together. His tongue flicks out for a second, licking a drop of energy drink off his moustache, then disappears back into his mouth.

I realise that I am staring at my uncle and drop my eyes to the carpeted floor.

"Oh John," Uncle Moses says, turning back to address Dad, "the boy is shy."

But I'm not shy. I'm just curious. Is something wrong with Uncle Moses's left eye? Does it keep twitching? Is it a little bigger than the right one? Or are my eyes just playing tricks on me?

Clearing my throat, "This is Babirye, her twin brother Kato, Kunda, and Sanyu," I introduce my friends.

Suddenly there is a beeping sound.

"What's that?" Uncle Moses says.

Dad gets his phone from his pocket. The beeping sound is a notification from it.

"Oh no!" he says, his eyes widening as he stares down at his phone's blinking screen.

"What's that bro?" Uncle Moses asks again, craning his neck to see what is on Dad's phone.

"It's a code-red alert," Dad says. "Something has gone wrong at the farm!"

Uh-oh! We're in trouble!

7

Dad rushes out of the house. He keeps his eyes glued to his phone as he bursts into the workshop. My friends, Uncle Moses and I are close behind him.

Uncle Moses asks, "Do you know what the actual problem is?"

"I can't be sure," Dad says, "but I think a plant pod has malfunctioned. I'm going out to the field to check it out."

"I'm coming with you," Uncle Moses says. "But what does a plant pod do?"

Dad searches his desk as he speaks. "It's a small, cylindrical reservoir for the three major plant nutrients: nitrogen, phosphorus and potassium." He stops searching and stares at his desk. "Where is that toolbox!"

"Maybe you should first turn off that beeping sound so you can think clearly?" Uncle Moses says.

"Oh, I'd forgotten." Dad turns his phone off.

I say, "I think I saw it on a table somewhere. Let me get it for you."

As I go around looking for Dad's toolbox, Dad continues. "Well, the plant pod basically regulates the quantity of nutrients that go into the soil. You set it up so that your plants get only the required quantity of nutrients, nothing more, nothing less. That helps you get the exact plant yield. Because of the plant pod, I can actually predict exactly how many tonnes of maize I'll have after harvesting."

"What happens when the plant pod malfunctions?" Babirye asks.

"Either the plant pod will release more nutrients than required or will suck out the nutrients from the soil," Dad explains. "It's like malnutrition in human beings. Eating too much leads to obesity. Eating too little leads to starvation and diseases. So, the plants can become sick. And some of my plants are starting to show symptoms of sickness. Tendo, have you failed to find that toolbox?"

I have already found the toolbox. I'm holding it in my hand. But I'm frozen by what Dad is saying.

Could Sanyu's accident have caused Dad's plants to become sick? What kind of sickness is it? Are all the plants going to die? I know. I'm a farmer's son who doesn't know a thing about farming.

I'm too scared to ask any question. I just quietly walk over and hand the toolbox to Dad.

"Are you okay?" Dad asks me.

I nod my head, then find my voice and say, "Yes."

Dad turns around and walks to the scooters. He picks up one and starts it. Kunda, Babirye, Kato, Uncle Moses and I each get onto a scooter. Sanyu just stays away like the scooters are infested with cockroaches.

Dad leads the way out of the workshop.

Then he stops so suddenly that I almost ram into him.

The havoc created by Sanyu is in front of us. Dad stares at it, a frown on his face.

I know that the farm is neatly gridded by tarmacked roads that crisscross through it. If you see it from above using drone photography, it is a geometrical marvel. But now, there is an ugly, unplanned, crooked path through the maize stalks.

"Whoa!" Uncle Moses says in his loud voice, "Did the plant pod do that?"

I wish my uncle could just keep quiet.

Dad slowly shakes his head. Finally, in a voice so low he's barely audible, he says, "Tendo, what have you done?"

"It's my fault, Mr Katende," Sanyu says. "I can explain."

8

Sanyu has crept up on us as we are looking at the destruction of the maize plants. No one heard her coming. So, when she speaks, everyone, including Uncle Moses, almost jumps off their scooters.

Sanyu tells us what happened and apologises profusely. Her voice is dripping with remorse. There are tears in her eyes and her lips are quivering.

When Sanyu is done confessing, a hush falls on us. The uncomfortable silence stretches on for a few long minutes.

Finally, I say, "We are so sorry, Dad. We won't do it again."

"I'm sure about that, son," Dad says. "From now onwards, none of you are allowed anywhere near my farm without my permission and supervision."

I'm too busy searching for tiny stones on the ground to respond to my father.

"Also, I think it's time for you guys to go back home."

We turn around to take back our scooters.

"Not you, Tendo," Dad says. "I need you to come and see the results of your handiwork."

I feel Babirye's hand squeezing my upper arm before she leaves. "Bye, Tendo," she whispers.

I've messed up big time. This isn't what I had planned on doing today. If only we had stayed at Uncle James's house, playing boring video games….

I try hard to swallow the lump in my throat. I fight back tears. I have to remind myself that I'm fifteen and big boys don't cry.

Dad restarts his scooter and races off to where the damaged plant pod is. Uncle Moses follows him. I reluctantly restart my scooter to follow them, knowing well what we'll find.

I turn my neck to look back towards the workshop to see my friends one last time. But they are already gone.

By the time I reach the accident scene, Dad is on his knees, unscrewing the plant pod. Uncle Moses is standing, watching, arms akimbo.

Dad examines the plant pod and shakes his head. "Do you see what you've caused?" he asks me.

The green fluid that was seeping from the plant pod has seeped into the soil. A hissing sound is coming from the plant pod. The surrounding maize stalks are starting to turn yellow from the roots.

"I'm sorry, Dad," I say again.

Dad sighs and says, "Apology accepted. I just wanted you to see the consequences of your reckless actions."

I don't have to say anything to that. I just kept my head low.

****

Later that night, there is a knock on my bedroom door. Then the door bursts open and Uncle Moses barges in. Everything about him, even the way he moves, is noisy.

"How is my favourite nephew in the whole world?" he says.

I sit up in bed. I've been trying to find sleep and now the chances of that happening has just flown out the window.

Uncle Moses sits on my bed so heavily that the springs in the mattress creak. Then he shoves a box into my hands. "Early Christmas present," he says. "I thought after today, I shouldn't wait until Christmas to give it to you. You really look like you need some cheering up. I hope this helps."

I hold the plain white, slender box in my hands carefully, wondering what might be inside.

"Go ahead! Open it!"

Excited, I fumble around with the box, break the seal and open the box. Inside is a black, seven-inch computer tablet. I already have a tab. Another tab is the last thing I want. I try to keep my head low to avoid looking my uncle in the eye. Maybe if he had given me a car or motorbike—anything that would be of more interest to a growing young man.

"Aren't you excited?" Uncle Moses seems to read my mind.

"Well, it's a really nice gift," I say. "I don't want you to think that I'm not grateful. But I already have a tab. It's not your fault, because there was no way for you to know that. But still, thanks."

"Pick it up and turn it on."

I'm not in any mood to appease my uncle. But if I indulge him a little bit more, maybe he will leave me to get back to looking for my sleep. I touch the sensor at the bottom of the tab, turning it on.

Uncle Moses says, "I took the liberty of uploading onto it some games I guessed you might not have played before. They are the latest."

The screen lights up and shows icons for a number of games, most of which I have never heard of. At least my uncle hasn't chosen games I already have. Now I hope they are as cool as the ones on my old tab.

"Select a game you'd like to play," Uncle Moses instructs.

I select a game without even reading what it's about.

Suddenly, the whole room is lit up, like the tab's screen is a projector.

My eyes widen and my jaw drops.

Suddenly I know what this tab is. I haven't seen any in real life, but I've read about them on the internet and for a while now, I've been gathering courage to ask Dad to buy one for me.

I reach out with my index finger and pierce the air, selecting an options menu. Suddenly, I am no longer in my room. I'm in another world altogether. This is way cooler than the virtual reality games that my friends and I play at Kunda's flat, or even the video games at Uncle James's house.

"Ever played a holographic game?" Uncle Moses asks.

9

I am awake all night.

By the time the sun's rays pierced through the curtains in my bedroom window, I was just getting started on my third game of the night. At first, it felt weird working with the holograms, but after a few hours, and now so used to picking up weapons and cars and new lives in the air, it felt more real than the furniture in my bedroom.

"Tendo?" Dad calls, poking his head around the bedroom door that is ajar. "Whoa! What's that?"

I keep firing from my holographic gun at the bad guys in the game.

Dad opens the door wider and enters. He stands for a moment, watching me. I can feel his gaze at the back of my neck.

Suddenly, the hologram disappears.

For a few seconds, I freeze, holding onto a gun that's no longer there, my adversaries vanished. Then I realise what has just happened. "What did you do that for?" I demand.

"It's ten o'clock in the morning," Dad says. "Won't you have breakfast?"

"Oh… okay."

"Did you sleep last night? I kept hearing voices in your room."

I start counting the tiles on the floor.

"I suppose your uncle's gift was too irresistible?"

"It's okay," I say, shrugging. "I know you don't like it when I play video games for too long. I just wanted to try out something new."

"Let me hope I won't have to confiscate it. Come down for breakfast. Maybe later you can have some sleep. You look horrible."

Dad leaves. I am irritated that he sometimes forgets that I'm no longer a kid that needs to be ordered around.

I stare at the tab my uncle gave me last night. Did I actually spend a full night playing with it? How can time run so fast?

Suddenly, I feel so worn out, as the adrenaline rush I've had throughout the night wears off. I drop onto my bed, not bothering to go downstairs for breakfast.

****

I dream I'm fighting with the bad guys. But this time it feels too real. Their bullets hurting me. I start bleeding. I feel weak and drop onto the ground. But the bullets keep coming. Thankfully, now that I'm on the ground, most of them wheeze past me.

But the pain is unbearable.

And the blood!

The blood is everywhere! My clothes are drenched in it. Is all this my blood?

And this time, no hospital buttons for me to tap so I can get new lives.

As I bleed, I feel life seeping out of me.

Then my vision gets blurred. And the bullets stop.

I try to cry out for help, but no sound comes out of my throat. It feels like a boulder has been placed on my neck.

One of the bad guys stands over me, his grotesque facial features contorted with hatred. His eyes burn through my skull.

Why have I been firing at this bad guy? And why does the bad guy hate me so much? Isn't it just a game?

The bad guy opens his mouth to reveal rotten teeth and a green tongue.

"DIE!" he hisses.

Then he shoves his big gun into my face and pulls the trigger.

Suddenly, I sit up in my bed, shuddering. My eyes are wide open, my whole body and the beddings drenched in sweat.

I pull in a deep breath like there is barely any air in my bedroom. Then I start heaving, trying to fill my lungs with as much air as I can.

Is this how it feels like to die?

As I reel from the nightmare, I check my chest, arms and legs. No bullet wounds. I am relieved to be feeling sweat, not blood.

Then the hunger sets in.

10

After a quick shower, I go down to the kitchen and make myself breakfast. The chef bot, a robotic cook, is already making final touches on lunch. The aroma of roasted chicken wafts through the kitchen, making my stomach rumble.

I am halfway through my bowl of Choco Pops when I remember that I haven't chatted with my friends since they left the farm yesterday. I get out my phone from the pocket of my shorts and find I have forty-three text messages from our chat group.

I scroll through them. The first few messages are of my friends talking about how sorry they are for what happened at the farm. Kato texted about how he knew it hadn't been a good idea to try farming, that they should have stayed at their home playing video games.

Then, sometime in the morning, Babirye asked, "Where is Tendo? He's been offline too long!"

"Maybe his dad has grounded him for what we did yesterday," Kunda suggested.

I take another spoonful of Choco Pops and read on.

I read a text from Kato: "I don't think so. He's never been grounded by his dad. His dad is cool."

"You mean he's not like Kunda's mother?" Sanyu replied, adding five hysterically laughing emojis, the ones with tears flying from their eyes.

Kunda's mother may win the prize for being the most absent parent in the world, but she knows how to keep tabs on her son, making sure that he never stays out later than the curfew time of 8 pm, eats a balanced diet and lays his bed. But Kunda is still the typical teenager, even when he acts younger than his age. So, whenever he doesn't toe his mother's line, he gets the most ridiculously long groundings.

One day, Kato stole fireworks from his father's lab. I don't know what Uncle James needed the fireworks for, but he's always carrying out the most interesting experiments. Kato called me to meet him at Kunda's apartment building because, at twenty-five floors, it was obviously taller than our respective double-storeyed houses.

That day's plot: set off the fireworks at midday. It would have been hard to sneak out of our homes into Kunda's apartment building in the middle of the night, past our curfews. We didn't even know how fireworks would look like in the middle of the day as opposed to night time, but it wouldn't hurt to try it out, would it?

Sanyu's family hadn't yet moved to Mukungu town, so our group still comprised of only me, Kato, Kunda and Babirye. I'm sure Babirye would also have wanted to join us on our escapades that day, but their mother was in hospital and Babirye was spending a lot of time at her bedside.

Kunda, Kato and I got to the flat rooftop of the apartment building, and after reading the instructions manual in the box, we ignited the first firework.

Then everything went wrong.

Instead of the firework shooting into the sky, it shot into some bedsheets that were on a clothesline, drying, and the bedsheets caught fire.

"Oh my god!" were the first words that came out of Kunda when he saw the fire. His hands were on top of his head, his eyes wide with terror. "I'm dead!"

Kato acted fast. He ran to a hose that was lying at the extreme end of the roof, opened the tap, and doused the sheets with water. The fire died in a minute.

But the fire alarm had already been activated.

"What are we going to do?" I asked the guys, trying hard to remain calm.

"We run!" Kato said.

And that's what we did. By the time the Fire Brigade got to that rooftop, we were already on the ground floor, mingling with the small crowd that had gathered, wondering what had caused the fire.

Later that day, a police officer knocked at Uncle James's house. We had left the fireworks box on the rooftop and it had Uncle James's address from when it was shipped to him. There was no denying that the only person who was young enough to steal the fireworks and cause that fire was Kato. Babirye had a water-tight alibi: although her mother had been sleeping the entire time she had been at the hospital, a number of hospital staff had seen her there.

To his credit, Kato insisted that he committed the crime alone, even after being questioned for over thirty minutes. How had he gained access to the rooftop of a private apartment building where he didn't stay? He'd hacked into the building's security system. Being the son of a scientist, the police had to believe him.

But Kunda's lawyer mum didn't believe that story. Without any evidence, she sentenced Kunda to a month's grounding with no electronics at all. Thankfully, it was only two weeks to the end of the holiday, so we got to see him when the school term begun, but even then, he left school as soon as the last bell of the day rang and went back to being grounded.

His mother is that strict.

As for me, my parents never even suspected that I would be involved in such shenanigans. And even today, even though I should be grounded, like my friends are suggesting, I'm not. I just had a long night and morning, undisturbed by my phone.

I go back to reading their texts.

"Guys, this is serious," Kunda texted. "Maybe we should go to the farm to find out if Tendo is alright."

"That's not a good idea," said Kato. "Remember how Tendo's father said that we shouldn't go there again?"

"That's not what he said," argued Babirye. "He only said we shouldn't be at the farm unsupervised. I think we can visit Tendo at home without going to the farm itself."

And the conversation continued. After some time, it changed from my problems to what we should do today. Should we go back to Uncle James's so that we can play more video games?

"No way!!!!!" Babirye texted. "I don't want to hear about video games ever again!"

I drop the empty bowl in the sink. I'm still hungry, but I decide to wait for lunch, which is about thirty minutes away.

"Hi guys," I text the group.

Babirye is the first to text back, "Tendo! Where have you been?"

"I see you guys missed me," I say.

"Hey! What's up?" says Sanyu.

"I'm sorry about yesterday," I say.

"It's alright," Sanyu texts back. "We are over it. It's just that now I won't get to learn how to plant stuff."

"Hey!" Kato texts. "Tendo, what have you been up to, man?"

I tell them about my new tab from my uncle.

"That's so cool," Kunda texts. "My mum said she'll get it for me when she comes back from her Japan trip. I can't wait. It takes gaming to the next level."

"That's right," I text as I find my way to a chair to sink into in the kitchen. "I stayed up throughout the whole night playing. It's awesome!"

"By the way," Babirye texts, "was it just me or does your uncle have something wrong with his left eye?"

Kato adds, "It kept moving weirdly! And I think it's slightly bigger than the right one."

"Yeah, I also noticed it," I text. "I'll ask him about it."

The chef bot puts a dish of steamed rice on the dining table. Today's lunch is early. I'm so overjoyed I want to hug the robot.

"How is my favourite nephew in the whole world?" Uncle Moses says, his voice booming throughout the whole kitchen. I haven't heard him come in.

I turn in my chair and force a smile. "I'm fine, Uncle. How come I'm your favourite nephew in the whole world?"

"Well, you are my only nephew, I guess that makes you my favourite nephew."

Well, you can't argue with that logic.

"But how come I don't know anything about you, yet you are my only uncle?" I ask.

Uncle Moses places his large right hand on my head, a gesture I hate because none of my parents has done it to me since I was ten. I'm too old for that. "That's why I'm here for the Christmas season. I'm going to make sure that we rectify that, right?"

"Okay," I say.

The chef bot adds bowls of vegetables and roasted chicken on the table.

"Should we wait for your father or can we start eating right away?" Uncle Moses asks.

Just then, Dad also walks in. His jeans are soiled at the knees. It looks like he's been working in the field since morning, most probably trying to reverse the damage we caused yesterday.

"No need to wait," he says.

When I sink my teeth into a chicken thigh, I realise that I've been starving. The Choco Pops barely filled my stomach.

rush back into my bedroom as soon as I am done with lunch. My uncle and father are still eating. I'm already missing my new favourite pastime.

Before I know it, Dad is calling me down for dinner.

"Tendo? Are you fine?" Mum asks me. She's seated across the table from me, eating a small salad.

Mum is a funeral director and she runs her own funeral services company. She is still dressed in black and her dreadlocks are tied in a tight bun, which means that she has just come back from work and hasn't gotten time to freshen up yet. She tries to be home in time for dinner at least twice every week.

I nod my head.

"He's barely gotten out of his room today," Dad reports.

"What's keeping you busy?" Mum asks.

Uncle Moses says, "It must be that new tab I got for him."

I quietly shove mashed potatoes into my mouth and swallow, barely tasting the food. I barely even notice what I am eating.

"Tendo," Mum says, trying to get my attention, "should I be worried?"

"No Mum," I say, my mouth filled with food. "I'm perfectly fine."

"I've seen this before," Uncle Moses says. "The boy is just taken up by his new toy. Give him a day or two. He'll be so over it he'll even forget where he put it."

The adults go back to their adult conversations and I go back to finishing my food as fast as I can so I can get back to my game. I left it paused and am dying to complete the level I'm at.

"Excuse me please," I say, pushing back my chair and getting up.

"You are not excused!" Mum says. "Sit back down and wait until we are done with dinner."

"But I need to go to the bathroom," I lie.

"I bet you do," Mum says, "especially given the way you've been eating like a glutton."

"Please? May I go?"

"Let the boy go," Dad says.

Mum glares at Dad.

I get up and push back the chair.

"You are not excused, young man," Mum says, turning her glare on me.

I walk three steps backwards, away from Mum's anger, which I'm used to. Then I turn around and run back up the stairs to complete my game.

I must have overheard Mum complaining to Dad about how he is soft on me, and how video games are not good for me.

But that is the least of my worries right now.

12

Days pass by in a blur. I'm too engrossed in the holographic games that I no longer text or call my friends. I don't even feel the need to go hang out with them. After the first day, they called me. I was too busy to hear my phone ring.

I'm barely eating or sleeping. I resort to sneaking snacks into my bedroom in the middle of the night to eat while I play.

The day I tried out the energy drinks that Dad forbade me to drink, it was like I had discovered the secret to living forever. Why did it take me years to try them out? Sometimes I'm too obedient to my parents for my own good. The space under my bed has turned into a garbage dump, littered with energy drink cans, candy wrappers and empty packets of potato crisps.

On the third or the fourth day—I can't remember—since I last saw my friends, Kunda's calls keep disturbing me so many times that I have no option but to pick up his call.

"Dude, what's wrong with you?" Kunda asks. He doesn't sound happy at all.

"Nothing. Why do you keep calling me?"

"Today is Kato and Babirye's birthday, but you seem to have ditched us! They didn't want to invite you to their party because you are not talking to them, but I convinced them that you would listen to me and you would come out."

I should admit that I have a crush on Babirye, in case you haven't yet noticed. I would want to think that I am the group leader, but Babirye most times is our leader, being the smartest of us all—that was until Sanyu came along and took over that title. I really like that about her. I haven't yet told her about my feelings for her. How do you tell one of your best friends that you have a massive crush on them? What if it destroys the dynamic in our group? What if it messes with our friendship?

Well, the one thing that is sure to destroy the dynamic in our group is me missing the twins' birthday party. It might even spoil my chances at ever asking Babirye out one day.

I look at my paused game. This particular level I'm at is quite difficult. I've failed it eighteen times. But I'm getting better. And I am sure in one or two more times, I will beat it and go to the next level. I have been improving with every trial. I can't wait to see what is at the next level.

"I'm sorry, Kunda, I can't come," I say.

"Is it that silly new game of yours?" Kunda asks. "Have you broken up with your friends for a tab?"

"No! Of course not! How could I do that to you guys? My dad grounded me. Didn't I tell you?"

"How could you have told us when you are not talking to any of us?"

"He had also taken my phone," I lie and feel a knot in my stomach.

"I'm sorry about that. I know how it feels like."

"Would you guys like to come over sometime and we play a holographic game together?"

"I'll talk to the others and see if they want to come. They are quite mad at you right now. And I can't blame them."

"I'm sorry. But now I have to go."

I hang up and go back to tackling the difficult level I'm at in the game.

At some point in the middle of the night, I drop onto my bed in utter exhaustion and black out. The nightmares come back, tormenting me in my sleep.

When Uncle Moses shakes me out of my fitful sleep, I scream. But as I gain consciousness, I realise that it is Uncle Moses waking me up, and not a bad guy trying to kill me.

"My favourite nephew," Uncle Moses says, his face too close to mine.

I can see lines of worry etched on Uncle Moses's brow. Uncle Moses's left eye looks even weirder up-close. It finally dawns on me that it is a robotic eye. White ceramic with the iris made of a lens.

"Were you having a nightmare?" Uncle Moses asks.

I nod, then ask, "What happened to your left eye?"

"It was an accident. Long story."

"I love long stories! Please tell me."

"Unfortunately, there's no time for that," Uncle Moses says, getting up from my bed. "Your friends are here to see you. Can I ask them to come up?"

I look around my bedroom. When was the last time I changed my sweat-drenched bedsheets? Why are my dirty socks and underwear strewn all over the floor?

"No," I say. "I'll be down in a minute."

Now, where did I put my phone?

13

I find my friends in the sitting room, listening to Uncle Moses telling them a story. Kunda is the first one to see me.

"Tendo," he says. "Why didn't you tell us you had a funny uncle?"

My uncle is funny?

"Where is Sanyu?" I ask.

"She is a little under the weather," Kato says, "but she doesn't want us to talk about it."

Kunda says, "I think she just wants to stay as far away from a farm as possible, lest something worse happens."

Babirye stands up and hugs me. "Oh Tendo," she says. "We are so sorry for being mad at you. We didn't know that you had been grounded and your phone was taken from you."

"Really?" Uncle Moses says, sitting up in his armchair. I notice that he is eating a slice of cake with a bamboo fork. "How come I, your favourite uncle in the whole world, didn't know that you had been grounded? When did this happen?"

"Er… um," I babble, about to break into a sweat. What can I say to get myself out of this tangle of lies? Now everyone is looking at me, waiting for me to explain myself. I shrug and say, "Well…."

"You weren't grounded?" Kato says, getting up from the couch.

This doesn't look good at all for me.

Babirye crosses her arms and glares at me, her angry eyes piercing holes in my skull. I don't think I am going to be able to ask her out any time soon. "What do you have to say, eh? You missed our birthday party, and we even saved some cake for you, thinking you were grounded, yet you weren't? What did we do to you?"

"This cake was for your birthday?" Uncle Moses asks, pointing at the cake with his fork, his mouth full of cake. Some buttercream is lodged in his bushy moustache. "It's delicious! Who made it?"

At that moment, Dad marches into the room and says, "Tendo! What have you done?"

I let out a loud sigh of relief at being rescued from that awkward moment by my father, but when I turn to look at him, I realise that maybe my troubles are far from over.

Dad looks angrier than my friends.

"What have I done now?" I ask him.

"You've been messing around with my robots!" Dad says.

"That's not true!"

Uncle Moses, with his mouth still filled with cake, says, "Tendo, lying isn't good. It is a crime." His voice comes out in an annoying sing-song.

"But I'm not lying!" I say. My fists clench and my chest rises up. "I have no idea what you are talking about! I've barely left my room!"

"Exactly!" Dad says. "You've been messing around with them from your bedroom! With that new tab of yours!"

"Is that why you didn't want to hang out with us?" Babirye says in a tiny, little voice. Her eyes glistening. This is no more the tom-boyish Babirye I know. Something about her changed from the time their mother passed away six months ago.

But now, just like in my video game, I am being attacked, and by none other than my own father!

"But that's impossible!" I shout. "All I did was play my games! How could that mess with your robots?"

"Don't raise your voice at your father, nephew," Uncle Moses says. He keeps calling me nephew, like that's my name. I am starting to hate it.

Dad tries to explain, "Obviously, your tab doesn't have all the computing power it needs to run the games on it. I think it is designed to find other computer systems on the network and piggyback on them. For a few days now, I've been noticing some malfunctioning in two of my farm robots. Then this morning they refused to start. I've done all the troubleshooting I know and nothing will work!"

"Maybe it's because they are old and need to be replaced?" I suggest. I've just started enjoying my games, and the last thing I want is to be responsible for any more damage on the farm. I can't imagine my tab being responsible for it. That means it would be taken away from me.

"I'm sure they are not old," Dad says. "While I was running diagnostics, I noticed that the problem was coming from one of the computers on the network, and when I searched for its location, I found that it was in your room."

"Could it be my phone maybe? It could be having a virus that's causing it to do all these things without my knowledge."

"You've barely touched your phone in the last few days. Yes, I can see your activity on the network. Your phone is even currently off. Its battery must have died. So that leaves your tab. I'm afraid I'm going to ask you to stop using it. I won't have my work disrupted like this."

For the second time in a week, I have been the cause of destruction at my father's farm. What's wrong with this holiday?

Uncle Moses gets out of his armchair, walks past me, and puts his arm around Dad's shoulders. "Come and show me what happened to the robots, brother," he says. "Maybe I can help with the repairs."

He then leads Dad out of the sitting room back to his workshop.

Silence hangs in the sitting room like a heavy, dark cloak. None of us could find something to say about what has just happened.

As I am composing the perfect words in my head to use to get my friends to forgive me, the doorbell breaks the silence.

I tap on a screen in the wall to see who is at the gate.

Why is Mr Makanika here?

14

Mr Makanika drives down the long driveway in his old, rusty pickup truck. My friends and I are standing at the porch, watching him.

He stops the old clunker in front of us and, with his elbow hanging out of the truck window, asks, "What has happened here, guys? You all look like you are from a funeral."

"Oh, nothing Mr Makanika," Kunda says. "We are very fine."

Kato, shrugging, says, "We are at the funeral director's home, so—"

I'm sure that was meant to be a joke, but no one laughs. Just six months ago, Mum had to organise his mother's funeral. It was the most surreal and awkward time of my life. We never talk about it, but I find it brave of him to be able make such a joke.

"What have you come to do, Mr Makanika?" I ask. I wonder if the robots have been destroyed beyond repair that my father has called Mr Makanika to take them to his repair shop, dismantle them, and sell their spare parts. That's how Dad always gets rid of his old farm equipment.

"I have some drones for your father," Mr Makanika says. "He always hires them around this time to help him get his maize ready for harvesting. Let me go right ahead and drop them off."

Mr Makanika drives off around the house to the workshop.

"Come on, guys," I say. "It's going to be fun watching my dad fly the drones and position them all over the farm."

I start running after Mr Makanika's truck, then stop. I look back. No one is following me. I am definitely no longer the leader of the gang. "Guys, come on," I say, motioning with my hand.

"We don't want to ever speak to you ever again," Babirye says, her arms folded. "How could you ditch us for a stupid game?"

I walk back to the porch where my friends are waiting. "I'm really sorry guys, okay? I know I messed up. I lied. But if you were the ones playing that game, you'd forgive me. It's hard to stop playing once you've started."

"So, you weren't actually grounded?" Kunda asks. "And your phone wasn't taken away from you?"

"No," I say. "I just have no idea where my phone is. And it's because of that game. We should play it together sometime."

Kato says, "But your dad just said you shouldn't play it again. It's spoiling his robots."

"We can figure out a way around it," I say. "I'm sure the game is totally harmless and this is just, you know, an unfortunate coincidence. But please, for now, come with me and let's see the drones."

"By the way," Babirye says, "I haven't yet forgiven you."

I give her a sheepish smile. She can't help but return it. My heart swells.

This time when I run towards the workshop, my friends are in tow.

Mr Makanika is off-loading boxes of drones from the back of his truck when we get there. There must be about twenty of them. "Give me a hand, guys," he says.

We go right to work, ferrying the boxes to a table inside the workshop.

I see my father and uncle on another table further inside the workshop. They are bent over a robot, trying to get it to work again. I feel bad for what I have done, even though I have no idea how a harmless game could cause so much havoc.

Kato, a box in his hands, is passing by me when he stops and whispers, "I think your uncle ate all the cake we had saved up for you."

15

"There!" Mr Makanika says, clasping his hands together and stepping away from the table with the robot. "I think it will now work. Turn it on and we see."

Everyone has surrounded the table on which the faulty robot lies. After Dad and Uncle Moses failed to figure out how to repair it, Mr Makanika offered to help.

Dad now turns the robot on. It sits up and lights up. It looks around, then jumps off the table.

Getting out his phone, Dad types in a few commands and the robot starts moving.

"It's working!" Babirye shouts, exhilarated.

"Thank you very much, Makanika," Dad says, shaking Mr Makanika's hand. "I don't know what I'd have done if you hadn't come."

"Well, I needed to deliver these," Mr Makanika says, pointing to the table piled with drones.

"Oh, yes. The drones. Thank you for them too. I'm sure I'll be done with them in three or four days."

"Uncle Katende," Babirye says, "what exactly do the drones do?"

"They help with drying the maize before we can finally harvest it," Dad says. He seems to be back to his normal jolly mood, now that his robot is working.

"How?" Babirye asks. She is back to being curious and inquisitive. It seems my transgressions have been forgotten by Babirye and my dad.

"They create an ozone layer around themselves to protect the plants from getting damaged by the harsh, harmful sun rays," Dad says. "Do you know what the ozone layer is?"

"Of course," Babirye says. "I'm not an uneducated chimp. It is a layer of a form of oxygen high up above the earth's surface that protects us from the sun's harmful rays."

"That's correct, Babirye," Dad says, beaming. "But you see, humans haven't taken good care of the earth. So over time, some parts of the ozone layer have been destroyed, creating what they call ozone holes. These drones offer an extra layer of ozone to protect the plants."

I roll my eyes. My dad should have become a teacher, not a farmer.

"Why do you protect the plants for only a short time?" Babirye asks, her forehead wrinkled in a frown, her hand on her chin. "If the rays are harmful, why not protect the plants all the time?"

"In some parts of the world, they use drones to protect their plants throughout the year. Here, our ozone layer hasn't gotten to that level of deterioration yet. But still, the plants are most vulnerable to the sun rays when they are very little, and when they are ready and have started drying. If I don't use the drones now that the maize has started drying, I risk having my maize catch fire."

"Can we watch them fly?" Kunda says, shifting his weight from one leg to another like he badly needs to use the bathroom.

"Sure," Dad says. "But it's not as fun as you would have liked. Most of it is automated. I could do it on my phone, but because you want to watch, follow me to my office. The computer there has a large screen."

Mr Makanika says, "I've seen this so many times. I don't need to stay around. So, goodbye guys. Enjoy your day."

Just as Mr Makanika is getting out of the workshop, he turns around and says, "Mr Katende, I'd forgotten, but I think I have something you might like."

16

"What is it, Makanika?" Dad says.

"A few days ago," Mr Makanika begins, "Dr James dropped some interesting equipment at my repair shop. They are machines that help create rain. I tried them out and they are quite impressive. I thought you might be interested in them this coming planting season."

"Are you talking about the Rainmakers?" I ask.

"Those ones," Mr Makanika says, turning to me and winking. "I'm sure your father will find them very helpful."

Babirye says, "But didn't Dad say that the government has refused to grant him a licence to use them and he wanted you to sell off their parts?"

Mr Makanika waves his hand like he is swatting away a fly. "I know what he said, but there is no way the government will know that some farmer this far in the north is using them. And I don't see why Mr Katende can't take advantage of them. He won't be harming anyone, will he?"

Dad says, "Thanks Makanika, but if James said they shouldn't be sold, then he had very valid reasons. I don't want to go behind his back and buy them."

"Then let me break them into parts which you can buy," Mr Makanika suggests, "then you can reassemble them here and use them. You wouldn't have gone behind your friend's back."

"It's the same thing, Makanika," Dad says. "And if the government won't permit their use, then there must be something wrong with them. I run a legitimate business here. So, unfortunately, I'll pass. Getting on the wrong side of the law is the last thing I'd like to do."

"Well, I was just helping," Mr Makanika says. "I'll offer them to another farmer who will find good use for them, and you'll regret why you didn't buy them when you start seeing other farmers having better yields than you."

Mr Makanika leaves and Dad motions to us to follow him to his office. "We have to get the drones up as soon as possible," he says.

"I can't believe Mr Makanika would go against Dad's wishes and sell the Rainmakers," Babirye says as she gets herself comfortable on a stool in Dad's office.

"But what's wrong with selling them if the farmer will be careful not to let the government know that they are using them?" Kato says.

"You have to always do the right thing, Kato," Dad says, "even when no one is watching. That's what having integrity means."

I don't think that lesson will sink into Kato's thick skull anytime soon.

As soon as Dad sits down in his chair in front of the computer, he hits his forehead with the palm of his hand. "Oh dear!" he says. "I forgot!"

"What?" Kato asks.

"We need to first get the drones out of their boxes and turn them on," Dad says. "Come on guys, let's go turn them on."

We follow him back out into the workshop.

Uncle Moses is already at work, unpacking the drones. "I thought you might need them out of their boxes," he says. "They can't fly while still in their boxes, can they?"

We all laugh.

Dad opens one of the boxes and shows us how to turn them on. We follow his instructions and in no time, all twenty drones are on, with red lights blinking.

"Now let's carry them outside so they don't have to bump into each other as they get out of the door," Dad says.

After all the drones have been arranged outside on the ground before the maize farm, we all go back into Dad's office to fly them.

Dad opens an application on his computer and the screen is filled with a map of the maize farm.

"All I have to do is select the points in the farm where I want the drones to hover," he says, clicking on different parts of the farm. "I just need to make sure that they are evenly spaced out. Now all that's left is for me to click on this icon and all the drones will automatically move into position, and that's where they'll stay for the next three to four days."

Suddenly, I get an idea. "Guys, I think it would be more fun to watch the drones flying outside instead of watching the little dots on Dad's computer moving around."

My friends and I dash out just in time to see the drones lift off the ground.

"Whoa!" Kunda says. "That's super cool!"

Leaning against the workshop wall, Uncle Moses also watches the drones take flight, but his face doesn't light up in excitement like ours. He seems to be deep in thought.

None of my friends seem to notice him.

But I do.

17

Later that night, after I have spent so much time catching up with my friends that I have stopped feeling guilty about ditching them for a few days, I retire to my bedroom.

For the first time, I notice the chaos I've created. The first thing that reaches my senses is the smell. I set out to look for it, sniffing around the room like a mouse.

I smell the rotten whiff first before locating the mouldy fried chicken thigh under my bed, an empty candy wrapper covering it from view.

How have I lived in this space so comfortably?

Suddenly, I am grateful that Mum no longer comes to my bedroom like she used to when I was younger. She used to give the excuse of needing to tuck me in.

I walk back downstairs and pick up a garbage bag. The cleaning that is required to get my room back to its original state is a lot. I'm too ashamed of myself to even use a robot to help me out.

An hour later, my bedroom is back to being habitable. The dirty clothes are out in the laundry room. The clean clothes are back in the wardrobes and drawers. The beddings have been changed for fresh, clean ones. I've finally found my phone in a sock and now it's wirelessly charging on my bedside table. I have no idea how it got into a sock.

My new tab is off for the first time, lying face-down on the bedside table. Next to it is my charging phone. Next to the phone is my old tablet. I had even forgotten that it exists.

I pick it up and turn it on. The wallpaper is an old photo of Kato, Babirye and me. It was taken about two years ago by the twins' mother on their birthday. I think their birthday two days ago is the first one I have missed.

I remember Uncle James made a huge deal out of that birthday two years ago because Kato and Babirye were finally teenagers. Some of their cousins from down south even travelled to attend the birthday party. You would be forgiven if you had crashed the party for the food, mistaking it for a wedding. There were lots of food and drinks. Of course, the alcohol was reserved for the adults only.

The photo I am looking at was taken while we were cutting the cake. Somehow, I was always part of the cake-cutting ceremony, like we were triplets. In fact, some kids at school have asked if we are triplets, given how we are always hanging out together and being all fraternal.

A few months after that party, the twins' mum, Aunt Karabo, was diagnosed with breast cancer. The next eighteen months were a gruelling rollercoaster of emotions, as she went in and out of hospital.

In that time, Kato became rebellious, getting himself into as much trouble as he could. Everyone said that that's expected of boys his age. I'm yet to experience such destructive urges like Kato's.

Babirye, on the other hand, suddenly matured, ditched her tom-boyishness, and started behaving more lady-like.

Although she remained inquisitive by nature, there was no more climbing through bedroom windows for her.

I guess it was this transformation that contributed to my finally starting to notice her as a girl for the first time in my life. All of a sudden, she was so different from us, the guys she hung out with, which made her attractive.

With two fingers, I zoom in the photo. Babirye is in the middle, Kato is on her left and I'm on her right. All three of us have those cheesy birthday cone hats on our heads. We also have silly grins on our faces. This is the last photo we took before Aunt Karabo was diagnosed with cancer and our lives changed forever. This is our last childhood photo.

I zoom in some more until Babirye's face fills the screen. She is beautiful. In the photo, her teeth have braces, but she had them removed almost a year ago. In those two years since this photo was taken, she has become even more beautiful.

I need to ask her out one of these days. The thought has been invading my mind more frequently lately. It feels like if I'm not playing video games, I'm thinking about Babirye, and plotting ways of telling her how I feel.

I've tried texting her a few times but I end up deleting the texts before sending them. Maybe I should video call her, see her facial reaction in real time. Better still, I could tell her in person.

But what if she turns me down. I think I would die.

My first idea of texting her is better. At least then, she will have some time to think about what I have written, and she will most likely text back her response. If it's a no, then I don't have to die in her presence.

But, if she were to say yes, then what?

I've never had a girlfriend before, so I don't know what to do. Do we make out? Do we more than make out. Kato and Sanyu have made out a few times, according to Kato's boasts, but I don't believe him. He is prone to lying and exaggerating stuff.

I can imagine Babirye and I making out. I've never kissed her, but I imagine her lips being soft and warm. As my mind goes to other things we could do, I instinctively inch my hand down my stomach, through the elastic waistband of my shorts, and I am no longer thinking straight.

Less than a minute later, I'm done scratching the itch, but this feels so off….

18

I try to think of ways to occupy my mind with something else, get it off what I've just done and the resulting shame. Maybe I should read a comic book off my old tab?

But can't the new tab also be used to read comic books?

Since I got the new tab, all I've used it for is playing holographic games. But I am sure it can do much more than that.

I pick up the new tab, turn it on, and go online. This shouldn't take up so much computing power that the tab needs to borrow other computers' power. The last thing I want is to get back into trouble with my dad.

I download the comic book reader onto the new tab and sign in to my account. I select the last comic book I read and I am automatically taken to the last page read. Just as I am starting to read my favourite comic book, a notification flashes on the screen.

"Play Incredible Combat up to Level 20 and stand a chance to win 20 extra points!"

I read the notification three more times, then swipe it away. I am not going to be tempted. Not tonight.

I go back to reading my comic book. It's an old Batman comic and I'm just getting to the more interesting parts.

The notification comes back again: *"Play Incredible Combat up to Level 20 and stand a chance to win 20 extra points!"*

I read it once and swipe it away. I continue reading my comic book.

Why isn't my favourite comic book as interesting as it was just last week? I've read enough comic books to know that I should be getting to the climax of the story, where it becomes unputdownable. But my mind just won't focus on the story.

When the notification comes back on, I almost swipe it away before reading it, only to notice that it is different and longer.

"If you don't play Incredible Combat up to Level 20 within the next 15 minutes, you stand to lose all the points you have accumulated and go back to zero! Play now before it's too late!"

I read the notification again.

And again.

This is unfair!

I look at the time, it is 10:30 at night. I'm on Level 19. It could take me about thirty minutes to get to Level 20 and earn the extra points, while at the same time saving the ones I already have from disappearing.

But Dad has banned me from playing these games. They have been causing destruction to other computer systems, or so he thinks. I don't believe him, but I don't want to go against his will.

The games have also caused me to start having nightmares. I hadn't had nightmares for years. I'd first had them years ago when I tried watching a horror movie and concluded that I wasn't excited by blood and gore. Reliving the horrors in the movie in my dreams had made such movies a total turnoff for me.

Now they are back. Different, but still as chilling. I can't deny the fact that they may have been caused by the holographic games I was playing because the characters in the games were the same ones terrorising my nights whenever I went to sleep.

My biggest challenge is that the games are addictive. Once I started to play, I wanted—scratch that: needed—to play some more. Every new level I get to demands that I finish it and get to the next one as soon as possible because, who knows what new thrills await me at the next level?

I swipe the notification away and try going back to reading the comic book. This time I'm going to be a good boy and obey my father.

The comic book is no longer making any sense to me.

"You have 10 minutes remaining before you lose all your points," says a new notification.

Surely, nothing catastrophic would happen in thirty minutes of playing, I argue with myself. But what if something bad actually happens?

I stare at the ceiling and weigh my options. With my new experience, I can make up the lost points within a day or two… but wouldn't that cause much more damage than I've already caused? Wouldn't it be better to play now?

Tendo, get back to reading your comic book, I chide myself. Getting to Level 20 isn't worth the repercussions of disobeying my dad. But if the last 19 levels have been increasingly epic, how much more epic will Level 20 be? What if I am missing out on the best experience of my life?

Surely, I can sacrifice thirty minutes of my time to try out Level 20.

What's the worst that could happen? Dad's robots can be repaired, can't they? Well, assuming there is some truth to what he alleges. And I know that he easily forgives and forgets. Won't he understand that I couldn't resist playing just one more level for thirty minutes?

Tendo, get back to reading your comic book.

I swipe the screen to the next page of the comic book. Read. Then swipe. Read. Then swipe again.

Five pages later, I realise that I have no idea what I have just read.

"Uurrrgggghhhh!" I grit my teeth and with eyes tightly shut, press my fingers on my temples. Frustration is eating me up.

I can no longer deny the fact that I am addicted to video games. This holographic video game, to be specific.

There is another ding on the tab. Another notification. This one is even blinking in red and the words are in all caps:

"YOU HAVE 5 MINUTES REMAINING BEFORE YOU LOSE ALL YOUR POINTS. PLAY NOW OR FOREVER LOSE YOUR POINTS."

I sit up in bed and initiate the game.

A hologram shoots up from the tab. I select the start button and within a few seconds, I am lost in the world I had sworn to myself never to return.

How had I deceived myself that I'd never play this game again. This is pure, mind-blowing fun! Unlike in real life, in this game, I am a superhero, saving the world from bad guys.

I don't hear the door bursting open and Dad marching into my bedroom. I keep playing.

Until my holographic game disappears.

"That's it!" Dad says, grabbing the tab and turning it off. "You are grounded! And I'm taking your tab away!"

I am disoriented at first. Is Dad a part of the game? And why is it suddenly so dark?

"What?" I say.

"I said, you are grounded and I'm taking your tab away," Dad repeats. "I won't have you destroy this whole place! No getting out of here for a week!"

"But what have I destroyed now? I've just been playing for a few minutes. And I was going to play only up to Level 20 for a few minutes. That can't cause any problems, can it?"

"Look around you!" Dad screams. I have never heard my father raise his voice like that.

I look around. "Why are we in the dark?"

"Because your games have shut down our electricity!"

19

"Hey! Guys! My mum finally bought me a tab just like Tendo's! Would you like to come over to my place and we take it for a ride?"

That's the first text I see in the morning. It is in our chat group, from Kunda.

I switch off my phone. I turn in my bed and cover my head with the duvet. I don't feel like getting out of bed today.

Last night's events come rushing back into my mind.

I'm grounded. Really grounded, not fake grounded like last time.

I have never been grounded by my father before. Only Mum is that strict. Dad has always been my buddy, saving me from Mum's wrath all the time. I'm an average teenager. I never get into too much trouble. However, last night, even after pleading and begging, Dad refused to back down.

It is one thing to be grounded during the school term. At least you can go to school and see your friends there. But being grounded during the holidays is much worse. There is nothing to do but stay home and try to entertain yourself. The vast estate that is our home makes the loneliness even more pronounced. And now, with my new tab gone, no other entertainment seems good enough.

Maybe texting my friends could help.

I reluctantly turn my phone back on and the notifications pour in. It is my friends texting on the group.

Kato: Yay! Congrats! When can we come?

Kunda: Now! I'm so excited!

Babirye: We'll be there shortly

Kunda: Tendo, are you also coming?

I stare at that last message for some time. My friends can see that I have seen the previous messages. I can't pretend like I haven't read them.

I type a sad emoticon, then add, "I'm sorry guys. I've been grounded."

"That's an old lie, Tendo," Babirye texts. "Find a new one."

"I swear this time I'm not lying," I say, then I tell them about what happened last night.

"I don't believe you," Babirye says.

I shelve my idea of telling her how I feel about her until further notice.

I turn my phone back off. I stay in bed until I'm too hungry to remain under the covers.

I'm absent-mindedly shoving Choco Pops into my mouth when it dawns on me that Kunda might also get into trouble because of his new tab. And if I got grounded for a week, he will get grounded until he is thirty years old! I'm mad at my friends for not believing me, but I need to warn them. I turn on my phone and text in the group.

"Guys, don't play that game!!!! It's going to cause other computer systems there to malfunction!"

I grab some more Choco Pops while glancing at my phone's screen every few seconds to see if anyone has seen the message and replied.

After five minutes, no one has seen it.

I call Kunda. His phone rings, and rings, and rings. Until the call is disconnected.

Are my friends ghosting me the way I had ditched them? Why won't they believe that I am actually grounded this time, and am not lying?

I call Kunda again. Still, no answer.

Then I call Kato. No answer.

I finally call Babirye and she picks up after the third ring.

"You are interrupting our game," she says.

"Are you playing with Kunda's new tab?" I ask.

"Yes! It's so much fun! Why didn't you tell us it was this fun! Now I know why you lied to us! Even I would lie to you if I had a game this fun!"

"So… you guys are not mad at me?"

"We forgive you. This one time. Come over and join us."

"I can't. I'm grounded, remember?"

"Seriously?"

"Seriously."

"Sorry, Tendo," Babirye says. "And I'm sorry I didn't believe you at first."

Her voice sounds like honey, and I want to tell her about it. Instead, I say, "It's okay. But you need to stop playing right now. You're going to spoil the computer systems at Kunda's place! And you know how Kunda's mum is like, a terror."

"I don't think so. We've been playing for a few hours now and everything looks perfectly okay."

"Didn't you see what my tab did to my dad's robot? Didn't you read my text about how it shut down our electricity?"

"Maybe this is a different tab. Now I have to go. I don't want to miss any more!"

Babirye hangs up.

She doesn't believe me.

She doesn't believe me!

I need to find a way to save my friends from that tab before it's too late.

20

tiptoe into Dad's workshop. I can hear voices. Dad is chatting with Uncle Moses.

"I can't believe what you've done with this farm ever since Dad died," Uncle Moses is saying.

"It's been a lot of hard work," Dad replies. "If only you'd stayed around, it would have been better than it is now. But you never liked farming."

"After seeing how you use technology around here to make work easier and faster, I think I like this type of farming."

Dad laughs. "You've always been the gadgets guy!"

"I think I'd like to stay and work with you. We could partner, just like when we were young."

"Moses, I don't think that can ever happen. Not after what you did."

Deciding that I have eavesdropped enough, I tiptoe back into the house. I would love to hear more of Dad and Uncle Moses's conversation, but time is of the essence. From the way they are chatting, they don't sound like they are about to get done. They surely won't miss me while they are doing some brotherly bonding.

I check my watch. It is 10:30 am. About two hours to lunch time. Two hours are more than enough for me. They won't notice that I am missing.

Rushing to my bedroom, I stuff my bed with an extra blanket so that in case someone comes in, they will think I'm in bed, sleeping. Then I get out my phone and place it on the bedside table. The last thing I want is for Dad to track me down using my phone, that's if he decides to check and see if his son is still grounded.

I run out of the house, down the long driveway, out of the gate, down the street, all the way to Kunda's apartment building. I could have borrowed one of Dad's electric scooters, but they are in the workshop, and Dad would definitely hear me starting one. By the time I get into the lift and punch the button for the twentieth floor, I am panting and sweating like I've just run a marathon. I run down the hall to Kunda's flat and ring the doorbell.

No answer.

I ring the doorbell again, this time leaving my index finger on the ringer for a good number of seconds.

The door finally opens. Kunda sees it's me and he frowns in confusion. "I knew you were lying about being grounded," he says.

"I wasn't lying," I say.

"Then why are you here if you are grounded?"

"Have you never sneaked out of home after your mother grounded you?"

Kunda just shrugs.

"Won't you let me in?"

Kunda stands aside and lets me enter. He leads me down a short hallway to the sitting room. I've been here countless times. I don't remember how Kunda started hanging out with Babirye, Kato and me. It's one of those friendships that just creep up on you and before you know it, you are the tightest of buddies. No explanation. No reason. Kunda always has the latest virtual reality games in town thanks to a mother who feels the need to buy them as a form of penance for never being around. Kunda has never met his real dad, but has gone through two step-dads. He once told me that he doesn't want to get another step-dad any time soon. It's been two years since the last one. So now, it's just him and his mother living in this flat.

The hallway is filled with pictures of Kunda at different ages. My favourite is a large digital painting of Kunda standing behind his sitting mother. He is smiling shyly but his mother has a frown on her face with a glare that can cut through glass.

"I came to warn you about your tab," I tell him as we get to the sitting room. "It can be dangerous!"

"Really? How?"

"How many times must I tell you what happened to my tab?" I ask.

In the sitting room—which is tastefully decorated with minimalistic wooden sofas, cushions and a rug in different hues of grey, and an enormous TV that almost fills one wall and makes the room look smaller than it really is—I find Kato, Babirye and Sanyu busy playing a holographic game. They don't even notice my presence.

"First stop the game and check your electronics, see if they are still okay," I tell Kunda.

Kunda pauses the game.

"Hey!" Babirye complains. "What did you do that for?"

Kato utters an expletive.

Sanyu sees me and says, "Tendo, I thought you were grounded."

"I had to escape to warn you guys," I say. "Any internet-enabled electronics might be in trouble if you keep playing with that tab. It uses other computers' operating power to be able to work effectively."

"I don't think this tab has tampered with anything," Sanyu says. She is the tech nerd in the group and I want to believe her.

"You guys were there yesterday. You saw what happened to my dad's robots."

"Give me a moment," Sanyu says. "Let me run some diagnostics on the systems here."

We wait and watch Sanyu working on her phone for two minutes. No one asks how she got into Kunda's home network. She always finds her way around the security of any system. If she didn't naturally have a good heart, she would have made herself and her family rich through cybercrime. But she sleeps in their flat's sitting room because she is too old to share a bedroom with her younger brothers or her parents. I haven't known her long enough but I can tell that she doesn't seem to care that in our group, she is the most disadvantaged financially.

"Nothing is wrong," she finally says.

"Tendo, what if your tab is different from Kunda's?" Kato queries.

I pick up Kunda's tab and look through it. "No, my tab is exactly like this."

"Then there is only one other explanation for this mystery," Sanyu says, raising up her index finger. "Someone is remotely accessing your tab and causing all the problems at your father's farm."

"Yes!" Babirye says excitedly. "That explains it! Oh, how I love mysteries! Why don't we go to the farm so we can figure out who is remotely accessing Tendo's tab?"

"You mean someone might be intentionally targeting my dad's farm?" I ask almost annoyingly, finding it a little too hard to believe.

"I'd rather stay here and play," Kunda says, pouting his lips like a cry-baby.

Babirye says, "Me too. But imagine if we had two tabs with holographic games! All we need to do is find out what's wrong with Tendo's tab, repair it, then be able to play with it! If we are right, we might end up catching an actual bad guy while at it."

"Let's go!" I say.

I really need my friends' help, especially Sanyu's.

But most importantly, I need to get back home before my father discovers that I am missing.

21

We can hear the sirens long before we reach the farm.

"Something is wrong," Babirye says. "Something is terribly wrong."

We break into a run. The gate to the estate is wide open when we get there, so I don't have to use my palm on the biometric scan to open it.

Now the sirens are even louder. The house looks alright. But then I see it.

Billows of smoke rise up into the sky from the back of the house.

The maize farm!

"Look!" Kunda says, pointing at the sky. "Something is burning!"

We sprint to the back of the house.

The sirens are coming from two fire trucks. A number of robotic cranes and hoses jutting out from their sides, blasting water at a fire in the maize farm.

I look up, but can't see through the smoke if the drones are still hovering over the farm. Aren't they supposed to prevent such an accident from happening?

I spot Dad, standing with Uncle Moses and two firemen who are controlling the fire trucks from their tabs at a safe distance. I go over to where they are. My friends follow me.

"Dad, what happened?" I ask my father.

"Where have you been?" he says.

"I've been in my room. I'm grounded, remember?"

"Don't lie to me boy! I'm done with your games! This time I'm destroying your tab!"

"But I didn't cause this!" I protest. "I wasn't even around!"

"Well, I don't know how you did it, but your tab is the one that caused the drones to crash and burst into flames, causing the fire! If I didn't have fire sensors on the farm, the fire brigade wouldn't have come in time and I'd have lost all my maize."

My mouth hangs open, I stagger backwards, suddenly feeling sick in my stomach and end up with my butt on the grass, dumbfounded. Is this one of those nightmares that I've been having lately? If it is, I want out. I want to wake up immediately and get back to normal life as I know it.

Is someone intentionally targeting my father's farm, trying to destroy it, and using my new tab to do it?

Who is it?

Why are they doing this?

There is no way this is the work of my tab. I wasn't even at home playing it when the fire broke out! Dad had already confiscated it, for crying out loud!

I take a few deep breaths, steady myself, and raise myself back up. "Dad, I need that tab back."

Dad glares at me, fire in his eyes. "Are you insane?" he says. "I told you I'm going to destroy it!"

"But if you destroy it, we won't find out what exactly is wrong with it so we can fix it."

"I don't need to know what's wrong with it. I want it destroyed."

"Don't you want to know who's behind these attacks?"

"You are!" Dad says, pointing a finger at my chest. "You and your tab!"

"But Kunda has a tab exactly like mine, and his isn't causing any problems."

"We're done having this conversation," Dad says and turns back to watch his burning maize farm.

I turn to my friends and shrug helplessly.

The fire has been contained now. It's impossible to see the entire farm from the ground, but I am hoping and praying that not all the maize has been lost. Smouldering embers remain of what I can see.

"What are you going to do now?" Kato asks me.

"I know where the tab is," I say. "Follow me."

We run to Dad's workshop. On getting inside, we go straight to the office in the corner.

"Thank goodness it's not locked!" I exclaim.

I look around Dad's desk, then rummage through the drawers. The tab is on top of some books in the lower drawer of the desk.

"Yay!" I say, punching the air with a fist, my other hand holding the tab.

"Let's get to work," Babirye says. "We don't want your father to find us in his office."

I power up the tab. "So, what are we looking for?"

Sanyu says, "We need to check the code that was used to build the operating system. Let's find out if there is anything that was added to it, or anything amiss."

"Give the tab to me," Babirye says, reaching for the tab in my hand. "I have a better idea. Let me see what I can do."

Babirye starts tapping on the tab's touchscreen. "I'm checking the tab's activity log to see if there is something fishy that happened."

We all look over her shoulder as she works. Her small fingers swiping and tapping on the touchscreen so fast I have a hard time following her movements.

"Whoa! You've got some impressive game statistics here!" she says.

I smile. My heart swells and I have to remind myself that this is the wrong place and wrong time. "Incredible Combat is hard, but not for me."

"Well, I need to get to the start of the activity logs. See everything that's ever been done on this tab. There's just too much activity!"

We keep watching as Babirye does her thing. Halfway through it, I stop understanding what she is doing. She keeps swiping and tapping for a few more minutes.

Finally, she says, "I know what's wrong with this tab."

"Tell us already!" Kunda says.

"Someone on the network has been accessing it remotely, using it to share computing power with other computer systems on the network, wearing them out. They've been watching you as you play. It's like you've been playing with them."

"Just like I predicted," Sanyu says.

Babirye shows me the tab. "For example, do you see this log from last night? It shows that someone manually sent you notifications so you could play. These notifications weren't automatically generated by the game."

"I know I'm not the one who was accessing my own tab remotely," I say. "And I don't think my dad would knowingly do it. That leaves Uncle Moses and my mum."

"Isn't it Uncle Moses who got it for you as an early Christmas present?" Kato asks.

I nod my head. Then reality dawns on me. "Oh dear! Is Uncle Moses the bad guy?"

Suddenly, there are footsteps in the workshop. And whoever it is, they are heading towards the office.

"Uh-oh!" I say.

Babirye throws the tab towards me. I shove it into the drawer where it has been and shut it.

The footsteps draw closer.

I look around the office. A large metallic desk takes up most of the space. Dad's office chair is behind it, and a book shelf is behind the chair. Nowhere to hide!

Damn!

"John, I need you to listen to me," I hear Uncle Moses saying breathlessly, like he's been running.

"No Moses," Dad replies him. "My answer is still no."

Dad and Uncle Moses are heading towards the office!

"You need me here, John," Uncle Moses says. "You can't deny the fact that this farm needs more hands on deck. You've lost control over it!"

Dad opens his office door and freezes. He looks at my friends and me, moving his eyes from one to the other.

We look like mice that have been cornered by a cat, with nowhere to hide.

"What are you guys doing in my office?" he asks.

22

Dad shakes his head and says, "You must be kidding me!"

I have just narrated to him what my friends and I have been doing in his office. I have explained our theory and how we have come to the conclusion that Uncle Moses is the one behind the attacks on the farm through my tab.

Uncle Moses bursts out into a loud laugh. "This is the most ridiculous thing I've ever heard! John, don't tell me you believe a word these kids are saying. I think they watch too many science fiction movies! Their imaginations are running wild!"

Dad keeps shaking his head, his face sombre. "I didn't know you'd sink this low to save your tab, son."

"That's not true!" I reply. I point at my uncle, "He's the one who gave me the tab. And I've heard him offering to stay so he can help you. He's not a good man, Dad. He is up to something! We need to call the police on him."

"Him giving you a Christmas present and offering to stay doesn't make him a bad man. It actually makes him a good man. And if I'm to believe what you are saying about Uncle Moses accessing your tab remotely, I don't think that's possible. Your uncle is on an internet fast."

"That's right," Uncle Moses says. "One of the reasons I came to my hometown was so I could take a fast from the internet and computers in general. That's why I didn't even carry a phone with me. I haven't used a computer since I came here. So how have I been accessing your tab remotely?"

I scratch my head and realise that I don't have an answer for that.

Dad gets the tab from the drawer and throws it down on the concrete floor. Then he steps on it with the heel of his boot, cracking the screen.

"Noooo!" I cry.

He steps on the tab again, cracking the screen some more. He steps on it one more time and it disintegrates into dozens of pieces.

"There's no more tab to try to save now," he says. "So, stop this madness right away or I'll ground you for a month." Then he turns to my friends and continues, "And you lot, I think you're past your curfew. You better run home now."

I keep staring at my destroyed tab as my friends shuffle out of the office.

I fight back tears. My father doesn't believe me.

"I'm so disappointed in you, son," Dad says.

Suddenly, Mr Makanika bursts into the office.

"Mr Katende," he says, clutching his chest and trying to catch his breath. "Mr Katende, I rushed here as soon as I heard what happened. And I'd like to assure you that it wasn't my drones! My drones would never do anything like that. You are the first farmer to use them this month and I serviced them before bringing them over."

"It's okay, Makanika," Dad says. "I know it wasn't your drones. We had an internal problem. But it's been dealt with."

Mr Makanika's breathing normalises. Then he narrows his large eyes and, lowering his voice, says, "Then please tell me that my drones survived this accident, because I need to deliver them to the next farmer in a few days."

"I'm sorry, Makanika, but your drones didn't survive the fire."

"What?" Mr Makanika says, raising his voice. "That's unacceptable! Those drones bring in more money for me than anything else at the repair shop! And the harvesting season has just started! What do you expect me to do?"

"My farm is insured. I'm sure the insurance company will cover your drones."

"Then what will I do in the meantime? Eh? Sit back as I lose money?"

"I don't know what to do for you, Makanika. I'm sorry."

"You better be! You better be sorry! I don't appreciate anyone messing around with my source of income! Especially not now, when I'm planning to propose to my girlfriend!"

My eyes widen in surprise. I can't imagine any woman falling in love with old Mr Makanika. "You have a girlfriend?" I ask.

"Shut up, boy!" Mr Makanika barks. "Your father just lost me a lot of money and I'm thinking of ways to make him pay!"

23

"I'm not a bad person, am I?"

"Of course not, Tendo," Babirye says. "You are a good guy."

It's morning, the next day. I'm on a video chat with Babirye. With my new tab destroyed, I'm back to using my old one.

Babirye has called to find out how I am and we have been talking for about thirty minutes already. She's such a sweet and caring girl. I am still gathering the courage to ask her out.

Since her mother died, Babirye has become reserved. I think this is the longest she and I have talked in six months. Before that, we used to talk for hours on end about anything and everything. We are best friends. Today, she has told me about how she worries that she might also get breast cancer in, like, twenty years. That, maybe if she studied medicine instead of computer science like her dad, she would hopefully help more people like her mum and maybe find a cure for cancer. She has also told me about how she sometimes cries herself to sleep, how she misses her mother more than she lets on. And how she doesn't know how to talk about all this with her father or brother because they all seem like they are in their own world, grieving alone in their own way. She is glad that she's finally gained the courage to talk about it with someone. As for me, I have mostly listened, because, what do you tell a girl who recently lost her mother?

Then, in typical Babirye style, she turned the conversation back to me, asking me how I've been. I've told her about the nightmares, and the binge-playing while binge-snacking. She has laughed at the fact that I had to clean my room in order to find my phone. She said that she's glad at least there has been some drama during this holiday, which has helped her get her mind off her mum and the thought of not having her around on Christmas, which is around the corner.

For the first time in over a week, I had a good night's sleep, without any nightmares.

From my first-floor bedroom window, I can see the charred remains of the maize farm.

"Do you think Uncle Moses is the one behind all the stuff happening at the farm?" I ask Babirye.

She shrugs. "I'm not so sure, Tendo. But something is definitely not right with your uncle. All these things started happening after he arrived. Coincidence? Also, I don't like the way he looks at me."

"How does he look at you?"

"I haven't yet figured out exactly how."

"How bad do you think yesterday's fire was?" I ask her.

"From satellite images I looked up last night, only thirty six percent of the maize farm was destroyed." Only Babirye would be caring enough to look up such things. "Your father has insurance coverage, so he shouldn't be worried."

"What does insurance do, by the way?"

"The insurance company pays you back after you've lost something. Of course, you need to subscribe to the plan first by paying a periodic premium."

"So, they'll pay back my dad's lost maize?"

"They'll most probably give him money equivalent to the maize he lost. Not actual maize."

"Oh…."

Outside, on the farm, the wind starts blowing. Then it starts drizzling.

"Hmmm… that's weird," I say.

"What?" Babirye asks.

"It's starting to rain outside. We're in the dry season, and according to the weather forecast for this month, we don't expect any rain today. It is supposed to only rain on the day after Christmas and on thirtieth. On the other days, it's supposed to be sunny. That's why my dad had got the drones. This week the sun was supposed to be at its hottest."

"How accurate is your father's weather forecast?"

"It has always been accurate for as long as I can remember."

The rain starts increasing in intensity. I am forced to get up and close the window.

Then it starts pouring down in torrents with hailstones.

"Something is terribly wrong," I say.

My bedroom door opens and Dad enters.

"It wasn't me!" I say, watching him for any signs of anger.

Dad shakes his head and walks to the window. He stands in front of it for a while, quietly watching the rain pelting the windowpane. With hands stuck deep in his pockets, he says, "I don't know what's wrong with my farm this week."

"I never meant to cause you any trouble, Dad," I say.

"I know, son. It's not your fault. But you need to be careful how you interact with technology. It can become dangerous if misused." He turns to my old tab on its stand, with Babirye's face filling the screen. "Isn't that right, Babirye?"

Babirye nods her head and says, "Yes, sir."

"It's very evident that your tab isn't the cause of this storm," Dad says, and I suspect that he is going to apologise for destroying my tab, but he doesn't.

I grab my phone and send a text to my friends' group: "Can you guys see the storm? It's huge!"

"Really?" Kunda texts back. "There's no storm here. The sun is out shining bright."

Sanyu texts, "How can there be a storm at the farm when it's very hot and dry here?"

"There is no storm elsewhere in town," I say and the realisation dawns on me. This isn't a normal, natural storm.

Rummaging through my wardrobe, I get out a raincoat. As I pull it on, Dad turns around with a questioning look on his face.

"Where are you going?" he asks.

"Out," I reply, "to find out what's wrong. It can't be raining like this at this time of the year."

"I know. Something is not adding up. But it's dangerous out there."

"Don't worry, I'll be fine."

"Are you sure you'll be all right?" Babirye asks. The concern in her voice warms my heart

"Don't worry about me. Talk later."

"Be careful," she says, and hangs up.

I can no longer sit back and watch as my father's farm gets destroyed. The remaining sixty-four percent of the maize is will be spoilt by this rain. It's no longer about me being cleared of wrong-doing and getting my tab back. That's no longer possible. I need to save Dad's farm and this is the only thing I can think of.

I pull up the raincoat's hood over my head and face the rain.

24

Climbing onto one of Dad's scooters, I ride out into the maize farm. The destruction is all around me. Parts of the farm have been razed down by the fire and the ground is black with ash. The plants that hadn't been touched by the fire are now bent over with the weight of hailstones. Some stalks are already lying on the ground, uprooted by the strong winds.

The howling wind keeps hitting me in the face. I have to wipe my face with my left hand while the right hand keeps the scooter steady so that I don't lose my vision from all the rain beating my face.

I ride for about fifteen minutes then stop. I am not going about this the right away.

If it was me, where would I put them? I wonder.

I have looked at the map of the farm so many times. I am now trying to bring it back to memory, thinking hard. Then I restart the scooter, turn right, and ride as fast as the storm will let me. Within five minutes, I find what I've been looking for, half-buried in the soft ground.

One of Uncle James's Rainmakers.

****

I have never seen a Rainmaker in action, but instinct tells me that there are more. A storm of such humongous proportions can't be created by one Rainmaker. Or can it?

With the farm's map still in my mind, I set out to look for the other Rainmakers.

Twenty minutes later, I have found all four, turned them off and piled them onto my scooter. However, they are so heavy the scooter starts struggling to move through the mud. Two of the Rainmakers fall off.

The storm dies. As abruptly as it had started.

Within a minute, the drizzle stops and the sun comes out, shining like it hasn't been raining at all.

I give up trying to lug all the Rainmakers through the farm to the workshop. I carry the two that can comfortably fit on my scooter and ride out to the workshop.

Dad and Uncle Moses are waiting for me at the workshop.

"What are those?" Dad asks.

"Rainmakers," I say.

Uncle Moses comes forward and touches the equipment on the scooter. "Wow!" he says. "These things are what caused the storm? John, aren't these the ones that Makanika wanted to sell to you the other day?"

"If they are the ones made by James, then they are the ones," Dad says.

"They are four," I say. "Uncle James said he'd made only four prototypes before the government refused to grant him a licence. We took all four to Mr Makanika's repair shop. So they must be the ones."

"Hmmm…," Dad says, scratching his beard. "Then how did they end up at my farm?"

"I have a good idea," Uncle Moses says. "Remember how Makanika said that he'd find a way to get back at you for spoiling his drones? Maybe this was his revenge."

"I'm going to go to the repair shop and confront him," Dad says. "This isn't how you treat a client."

"I'm coming with you," Uncle Moses says.

"Me too," I say.

"You can't go, Tendo," Dad says. "Look at yourself. You are all drenched. You need to change your clothes and take some hot chocolate before you catch a cold."

"Then I'll go change right away. The hot chocolate can wait. The sun is out. It will warm me up."

"Okay. Hurry up. In the meantime, I'll go get the other two Rainmakers. Where did you drop them?" Dad asks as he straddles a scooter.

I tell him where I left the Rainmakers that had been too heavy for me to carry on my scooter. Then I dash to my bedroom and change into fresh clothes. As I am running back down the stairs, I stop.

My phone! I need to tell my friends what has happened.

I rush back, pick it up and run back down. My father and uncle are already in the double cabin truck, seated at the front, waiting for me. They have put the four Rainmakers in the bed of the truck.

I climb in the backseat of the truck.

Fishing out my phone, I text my friends, "Guys, guess what? We found Rainmakers at the farm! They caused a huge storm! We are now going to Mr Makanika's repair shop. We think he's the one who put them there."

Babirye texts, "Why would Mr Makanika put Rainmakers at the farm?"

I tell them about how Mr Makanika came to the farm after they had left and threatened Dad because his drones had been destroyed.

Kunda texts, "Maybe Mr Makanika has been the bad guy we've been looking for all along."

"He couldn't have started that fire," Babirye says. "He had his drones at the farm."

"What if his drones were old and he needed new ones?" Kato texts.

"Why not just go buy new ones?" Kunda says.

"Then he'd have to use his own money," I say, texting fast as Kato's theory starts making sense to me. "But if the drones got destroyed at my dad's farm, then he'd make my dad pay."

I catch Uncle Moses staring at me through the side mirror of the truck. He smiles and says, "Ah, teenagers and their phones! You would think they are an extension of their arms, a vital part of their body."

It's a short drive to Mr Makanika's repair shop but Dad is concentrating on the road. Main Street is busy.

I ignore my uncle and look back at my phone to see what my friends are texting. There are two unread texts:

"Then why did he start a storm at the farm?" Babirye asks.

"Maybe because Tendo's dad had refused to pay him quickly?" Kato says.

"Guys, I've got to go," I text. "We've reached the repair shop."

"We're also coming!" Babirye texts.

I pocket my phone and get out of the car.

25

Mr Makanika must have seen us through the window of his office. As soon as we drive into his repair shop, he comes out and says, "Mr Katende, have you come to talk about paying for my drones that got destroyed yesterday?"

"Don't worry about them," Dad says. "I already put in a claim with my insurance company. And they pay quite fast. In a day or two you'll have new drones. Today, I've come to buy the Rainmakers. You told me that they were on sale, right?"

"That's right," Mr Makanika says, winking. "I'm so glad you finally came around. These babies are the real deal. Just follow me. They are somewhere out here in the back."

We all follow Mr Makanika as he leads the way to the back of the repair shop. I can't help but wonder at how Mr Makanika can keep a straight face yet he knows very well that the Rainmakers are not at his shop.

"Tendo!"

I turn and see Babirye, Kato, Sanyu and Kunda running towards us. They must have been at Kunda's home playing with Kunda's new tab. That's the only way they could have got here that fast.

"Shhh!" I say, putting a finger on my lips to signal my friends to keep quiet. The last thing I want is for them to start talking about what we have just been texting about a few minutes back.

Mr Makanika suddenly stops and puts his hands on his head. His eyes, which are almost popping out of their sockets, are staring at an empty space on the industrial steel shelf. "Where are my Rainmakers!" he shouts. "I swear they were here last night when I closed shop!"

"They are actually in the bed of my truck," Dad says. "I got them from my farm where they caused a lot of damage to my plants."

"What?" Mr Makanika says, shaking his head in disbelief. "That's impossible."

"That's what I also thought. But would you like to explain to us why your Rainmakers were at my farm, causing it to rain down cats and dogs on my crops?"

"Are you saying I'm the one who put them there? Now why would I do such a thing?" Mr Makanika looks flabbergasted. If, indeed, he is the one who put the Rainmakers at the farm, he is a pretty good actor.

"You tell me!" Dad says, raising his voice. He has been raising his voice a lot lately.

Mr Makanika scratches his beard as he looks up at the iron sheet roof.

"Yes! I know what must have happened!" Mr Makanika finally says. "Someone must have stolen them from here and taken them to your farm."

"Why would someone steal from a repair shop selling old, substandard, outdated equipment?" Uncle Moses asks.

"That's a good question to ask," Mr Makanika says. "Anyway, like I was saying, someone stole them. And I have security cameras! Let's go to my office and check the footage. We'll know who stole them and we'll deal with this misunderstanding once and for all."

Mr Makanika leads the way to his office.

Babirye whispers to me, "I think Mr Makanika is telling the truth."

"I'll believe him when I see that footage," Kato says.

Mr Makanika's office has undergone a major transformation from the last time I saw it. Although it is still cramped, its metallic walls now have a new coat of cream paint. There are plastic flowers in a vase on Mr Makanika's desk. And the old, worn-out couch has a new cover. Maybe Mr Makanika really has a girlfriend after all.

All eight of us pack ourselves into the office as Mr Makanika boots up an old computer that looks like it is from the previous century. Within a few seconds, we are staring at the security camera recordings from the previous night. The screen is split in four quarters, each one showing different views of the repair shop, but with the same time stamp.

"I left this place at nine," Mr Makanika says. "So, the robbery must have occurred afterwards." He fast-forwards the footage to after nine. Then he keeps it in fast-forward mode, but not as fast as before. He sits forward in his rickety swivel chair, squinting his eyes so he can catch anything amiss on the footage.

Suddenly, the screen goes blank.

"What happened?" Dad asks.

"I don't know!" Mr Makanika says.

Sanyu says, "The cameras were turned off."

26

"How convenient!" Uncle Moses says.

"Are you saying I'm the one who turned my own cameras off so that they don't record the robbery?" Mr Makanika asked.

"No," Uncle Moses says. "I'm saying that you conveniently turned off your cameras so that if we came asking, you would have a very convenient story. You stole from your own shop, then installed the Rainmakers at my brother's farm. Admit it!"

"That's preposterous! I have no reason to want to cause any havoc at Mr Katende's farm!"

"Maybe you were angry that he had spoilt your drones."

"Would destroying his farm bring my drones back? And hasn't he promised to pay them back?"

"Then why did you threaten to revenge?"

"Are you mad?"

"Gentlemen," Dad says, raising his hands and getting between the two men before they can start exchanging blows. "Calm down. I'm sure we can resolve this like civilised people." Then, turning to my friends and I, who are watching the drama unfold, Dad lowers his voice and says, "Uh, guys, why don't you leave us alone for a few minutes?"

I grumble under my breath as my friends and I leave the room.

"I think Mr Makanika did it," Kato says once we are out of earshot of the adults.

I kick an imaginary pebble on the ground as I pace back and forth across an aisle lined with washing machines from the previous decade, my hands in my pockets. I bite my lip. My mind is racing. We don't have any real evidence that it was Mr Makanika who brought the Rainmakers to the farm apart from the fact that he'd been the one with them before last night. What if someone actually stole the Rainmakers, like Mr Makanika said? Could it be the same person who had been accessing my tab remotely to cause havoc at the farm? If it wasn't the same person, did that mean that the storm wasn't related to the power outage and the robots getting spoilt? Could it be Uncle Moses? But if it was Uncle Moses, how could he have done it? And why would he want to destroy his brother's farm?

Where was Uncle Moses last night?

My friends are arguing amongst themselves about who the bad guy could be, and they are now also thinking that it could have been Uncle Moses.

I finally stop pacing in front of them and say, "If it is Uncle Moses, I know how we can find out."

Now that I have my friends' attention, I get out my phone and continue, "With my phone, I can access the network at home and find out if anyone got out of the gate late in the night."

I access my home network and check the gate security system. Given that almost everything at the estate is computerised, from toilets to fridges, combine harvesters, gates doors and even to the curtains, it is easy to find out what has happened to everything from the convenience of one of the connected computers, tabs or phones.

"The gate was opened and closed at 21:45 last night!" I say, excited. "And it was opened and closed again fifteen minutes later! Someone went out of the estate at around the same time someone was stealing from Mr Makanika!"

"It could be a coincidence," Kato says.

"Hmmm…," Babirye says, stroking her chin. "It could be. But the timing is very suspicious. And there have been way too many coincidences lately. Tendo, can you access the cameras at the gate? Maybe we can see who it was that got out."

I tap a little more on my phone. "Surprise! Surprise!" I say.

"Who is it?" Kunda asks.

"The camera footage at the gate has been deleted as well!"

"Then whoever left your home last night is most probably the same person who stole the Rainmakers!" Kunda says.

"Exactly!" I say. "And I don't think it's anyone else apart from Uncle Moses."

"Hold on," Sanyu says. She has been quiet this whole time. "There is another possibility. What if the gate opening and closing the first time was because someone was coming in, not going out."

"That's a good point," Babirye says.

"That person would need to either have their palm registered in the security system, or know the security code for opening the gate," I say.

"Would you like me to hack into your home network right now and open the gate for you?" Sanyu asks.

"I believe you can. But no way Mr Makanika would have done that. I don't think he can. Can he?"

"Nothing is impossible," she says.

I sigh and put up my hands. "I can't dispute that," I repeat. "But between Uncle Moses and Mr Makanika, I would go with Uncle Moses. And Mr Makanika is too nice to do this."

Kato says, "How could he have carried all four Rainmakers? They must have been too heavy to carry from the repair shop back to your home."

"That's an important point," I agree, and I start heading to the car. "I bet he used my dad's truck."

My friends follow me to the car. We get in and I turn on the car's dashboard computer. It also shows that the activity logs for last night have been deleted.

"Mr Makanika has his own truck," Kato says. "No way he would need your dad's truck. Guys, I think we just confirmed who our bad guy is."

"This guy really covered his tracks!" I say, sitting back in the driver's seat of the truck.

Babirye says, "The fact that he covered his tracks is evidence enough for us. If he didn't have anything to hide, he wouldn't have covered any tracks!"

"And he did a bad job of covering them," I say. "He forgot about the activity logs of almost everything at home, especially the opening and closing of the gate."

Sanyu says, "Let's go back to Mr Makanika's office and ask Tendo's uncle where he was last night."

27

"Where was I last night?" Uncle Moses asks incredulously. "What kind of question is that?"

We are all back in the cramped office.

"Tendo, I thought you had stopped accusing your uncle falsely," Dad says.

"But all the evidence points towards him," I say.

"This is unbelievable!" Uncle Moses shouts. Then he lets out a scream and his hands fly to his left eye. "Awww!"

Dad goes to his brother and holds him. "Moses!" he says. "What's wrong?"

"My eye!" Uncle Moses says, writhing in pain. "Aw! My eye! It hurts."

Suddenly, Uncle Moses's eyes—the right one bloodshot, the left one actually bleeding—focus on Sanyu.

Sanyu doesn't seem to notice what is going on around her. Her eyes are glued to her phone and she is typing on it furiously. Her jaw is set and her brow wrinkled.

"Aaarrgh!" he screams and lunges at her. "What did you do that for?"

"Sanyu!" Babirye screams.

Then all hell breaks loose.

Sanyu's phone hits the floor and slides out the door. I jump for it.

Kato and Kunda fight the big, burly man off Sanyu. Babirye's scream is deafening. Mr Makanika barks commands about them taking their fight outside.

"Stop it!" Dad shouts, his fists clenched but limp at his side. "I said stop it at this very moment!"

It is a tangle of legs and arms on Mr Makanika's office floor.

Finally, Mr Makanika and Dad join in the scuffle and overpower Uncle Moses. He stands up and gives them all mean looks. Then he bolts out of the office like it is on fire.

"Don't let him get away," Sanyu says. "He's guilty of everything, and I can prove it."

"How?" Dad says.

"His left eye is a robotic eye. I hacked into it with my phone and retrieved something you might want to see."

"He's getting away!" Mr Makanika says.

Dad sinks into the old couch, suddenly tired. "Let him go. But I want to see what you have, Sanyu."

"Hold on!" Mr Makanika says, stretching out his hand. "Did you just say robotic eye? What in the world is that?"

"It's a prosthetic eye," Sanyu says, "it's just that this one is computerised. It's like a mini-computer inside your head. Mr Katende's brother had a robot put into his eye socket, where his left eye had been. A robotic eye actually works better than a real eye."

Mr Makanika sits back down in his chair and whistles. "Continue please."

"While Uncle Moses deleted his activities from other computers, he overlooked the computer in his head. I don't think he expected anyone to check it."

"I didn't even know it wasn't a real, natural eye!" Kunda says.

"Hacking into it wasn't that hard," Sanyu adds. "Robotic eyes are still a new invention, barely a year old. Their technology hasn't been refined well enough, so they are still prone to attacks. So, I attacked his eye and copied out his whole hard drive. Wait, where is my phone?"

"I have it," I say, handing it over to her. "Dove for it like a goalkeeper. If he had laid hands on it…."

"The hacking… it looked really painful," Babirye says, flinching.

"It wasn't my intention to hurt him," Sanyu says, and I can feel the remorse in her voice. "But anyway, I have some information that you should see. His eye keeps a record of everything he sees. Also, it's what he used to remotely access Tendo's tab without needing to use an actual computer. It looks like he'd programmed the tab so he could easily access it whenever he wanted long before he gave it to Tendo."

"I knew I was right about him!" I say.

"You were going to show us something, Sanyu," Dad says.

"Oh, yes," Sanyu says. "Permission to use your computer, Mr Makanika?"

"It's all yours," Mr Makanika says, vacating his chair.

Sanyu sits down in front of Mr Makanika's computer and begins accessing her phone's hard drive from it. We all gather around her so we can see what is on the screen.

Sanyu starts playing a video. "This is from last night," she says. "I thought you should see what you couldn't see when Mr Makanika's cameras were disabled. By the way, I think he used his robotic eye to disable them. He used that eye to do a lot of things."

On the screen is a grainy video, showing the repair shop. It is like whoever shot the video is holding it in front of their face and moving around with it. Of course, we now know that it was from Uncle Moses's robotic eye.

The video shows the Rainmakers on the shelf in the repair shop. Then two burly hands reach out and carry two of the Rainmakers, turn around, and carry them to a truck. It's undeniable that the truck is none other than Dad's truck. A few seconds later, those same hands carry the other two Rainmakers to Dad's truck.

"There are hundreds of hours of footage," Sanyu says, "but some of it shouldn't be watched by anyone younger than eighteen."

"That's enough, Sanyu," Dad says. "I've seen enough."

He goes back and slumps in his old spot on the couch. His brow is wrinkled and he looks like he has become ten years older in a few minutes.

"I wonder why he did all this," I say.

"I think I know why," Dad says, looking up at me with sad eyes.

28

"Why did he do it, Dad?" I ask.

"It's a long story, son."

Mr Makanika opens his mini fridge and says, "I have drinks. So, there's nothing stopping you from telling us your long story, Mr Katende."

Dad gives Mr Makanika a tired smile and asks, "Does this mean you forgive me for thinking you are the one who used the Rainmakers to destroy my maize farm?"

"Just tell us the long story and I'll forgive you," Mr Makanika says, handing him a soda. "But that doesn't mean I've forgotten about my drones."

Dad opens the can of soda and takes a swig. "Don't worry. You'll get back your drones. I promise."

Kato and Kunda sit cross-legged on the floor with sodas in their hands. Sanyu remains seated in Mr Makanika's swivel chair but turns it around to face my dad. Mr Makanika joins my dad on the couch. I lean back against the wall, my left leg bent, with the foot planted on the wall. Babirye comes and joins me in leaning against the wall, her arm brushing against mine.

"Damn!" Babirye says, her voice so low that only I can hear her. "And the plot thickens."

"Why did he do it, Dad?" I ask again.

Dad takes one more sip of his soda and says, "When our father died, he left us with the farm. It was much smaller than it is today. And of course, at that time, there wasn't as much technological advancement in agriculture as there is today. Moses wasn't interested in farming at all, so he left all the work to me. But after every season, he expected us to divide up the profits in half, even though he hadn't done anything to earn his half. I wouldn't have minded giving him some of the money I made on the farm. But he never agreed to anything I suggested. He kept wanting more money, yet he refused to reinvest the profits so that we could expand the farm and even make more money from it.

"We kept fighting for over a year until I couldn't handle it any more. I offered to buy him out. Each of us owned half of the farm. So, I offered to buy his other half. I ended up paying twice the value of his half of the farm, just so I could get rid of him."

"Man!" Mr Makanika exclaims. "That's like being a tick on a cow, sucking out as much blood as you can until you burst!"

"He has always been a bad guy," I say. "So why didn't you believe me at first when I told you he was the one using the tab to cause the destruction at the farm? It's quite evident that all these troubles started after he came."

"I'm getting to that part of the story," Dad says, then takes a sip of soda.

"Can I have some more soda?" Kunda asks.

I'm barely halfway through mine but Kunda already needs another one?

"Just one more," Mr Makanika says, handing him another soda.

Dad continues, "When he left, I never heard from him again. For years, I tried getting in touch with him, but I failed. I didn't know where he had gone. I started regretting why I'd suggested that I buy him out. I now had the farm, but I had lost my brother, my only living relative at the time.

"So, when he contacted me last month, asking if he could come over for the Christmas holiday, I was excited. I thought that I'd reunite with my brother. I quickly forgot about how he had manipulated me. I believed that he had changed. So even when you guys told me about him being behind the attacks on my farm, I didn't want to believe it. He'd been offering to come back and help out with the farm. From the conversations we have had in the past few days, I can now see that he intentionally wanted to destroy my farm so I could turn to him for help. I can only assume that he planned on taking control of the farm from me after some time."

Kunda throws back his head and shakes his empty soda can over his open mouth, with the tongue out, to catch any remaining droplets of soda. Then he says, "Wait, so this guy wanted to create the problems, then offer the solutions and come off as the good guy?"

Babirye frowns and asks, "Why wouldn't he offer to help you, just like normal people do?"

"That's what he first did, but I refused, because I didn't want to get into trouble again with him. I wanted to have my brother back in my life, but I didn't want him as a business partner. I just didn't know that he'd go to all the trouble he went to so that he could convince me that I badly needed his help. Sometimes love blinds you to people's vices."

"That explains why you'd barely told me anything about him," I say.

"I thought that I would never see him again. And I didn't want you to think that you had an uncle out there with questionable morals. Can you believe I found a few logged entries to my office that I couldn't explain? I thought that maybe I'd forgotten about being in my office, or you'd been in there goofing around without my permission. I didn't want to think of the possibility that my brother could gain access to my office. I wonder what he did there."

29

Uncle Moses has disappeared. Dad has even filed a police report so they can look for him, but they have failed so far. They can't even find him online. His phone numbers are disconnected. It's like he never existed at all before coming over to our home.

That afternoon, when we get back home, Dad and I head for Uncle Moses's room and find that he's left his luggage behind. On searching through it, we don't find any clues that can point us to where he could have gone or where he'd come from.

We later find out that Uncle Moses had tried gaining access to Dad's office computer one last time after running from Mr Makanika's repair shop. Dad's office computer has most of the important documents and agricultural inventions that he uses to run his whole business. If we hadn't found out about Uncle Moses, and foiled his plans, he would have kept trying, and maybe finally got through the tight security on the computer. Some of the technology my father uses on his farm is proprietary and he paid a lot of money for it. If my uncle had got his hands on it and been able to pirate it, I can only guess what he would have done with it.

I realise that throughout my uncle's stay at the farm, I didn't find out anything about him. What did he do for a living? Where did he stay? Did he have a wife and children? He always found an ingenious way to dodge any personal stories, hiding behind fake chumminess. Maybe he shared his story, whether true or made up, with Dad and not with me.

The farm is back to its normal operations. Dad lost all of his maize for that season, to the disappointment of all his clients. What hadn't been destroyed by the fire was destroyed by the rainstorm. But the insurance company has compensated him, and he is now planning for the next planting season.

My friends and I finally got to do some farming at the farm, with Dad's supervision of course. We have planted some beans and it is a delight watching them grow. Sanyu is the most excited of us all.

Mr Makanika has his new drones, although he keeps complaining about the one farmer who missed out on using them and how he lost out on making that money. That farmer's plants didn't get burnt by the sun's rays, so maybe he didn't actually need Mr Makanika's drones after all. Now, Mr Makanika must be worried that he might lose future revenues from that farmer and maybe even more farmers, if they start thinking that Mr Makanika's drones are more of a luxury than a necessity.

On getting back the Rainmakers, Mr Makanika broke them apart into pieces, and that's how he is selling them now.

My grounding has been lifted, but I still complain. "I can't believe you destroyed my tab," I keep reminding Dad.

"Alright, I'll buy you another one. Now stop whining!"

"But now I'll have to start from scratch, accumulating points in the games."

"Don't worry, you are not alone. Even I am starting from scratch on my farm."

"But you always start from scratch every season."

"That's life, son."

****

Lately, we have been spending our days at Kunda's flat, playing with his tab. Having had lots of experience from my own tab, I keep beating my friends. They keep begging me to teach them how to play like I do.

We keep badgering Sanyu to show us the explicit content in the videos she got from Uncle Moses's robotic eye, the ones we are too young to watch, according to her. She keeps fobbing us off. Even Babirye has suggested that Kato, Kunda and I are planning on hacking into her phone so we can view them. But finally she says that she has deleted them. Too bad.

On Christmas eve, while playing a holographic game at Kunda's place, Babirye starts screaming, "I have an idea! I have an idea!"

Kunda is forced to pause the game. "What is it?"

We have no option but to pay attention.

"Remember how my dad said that he couldn't get a licence for the Rainmakers because the government thought that people would end up stealing rain from one part of the country to another, which wasn't fair?" Babirye says, speaking very fast.

"Get to your point already!" Kato says. "I'm about to beat you guys at this round!"

"That's what the Rainmakers should be doing!"

We just stare at her, not grasping what in the world she is talking about.

"There are places which don't need rain, so the Rainmakers can be used to redirect rain to places that need it. For example, do you know that place in the east where every year it rains so hard that there are floods and landslides?"

"Around Mount Elgon?" I ask.

"Yes," Babirye replies. "So, the government can actually use the Rainmakers to move the rain from that place and maybe take it to Lake Victoria."

I nod my head and say, "That's brilliant."

"I keep telling you guys that my sister is very smart but you don't believe me," Kato says.

Babirye pokes him in the ribs with her elbow.

"Ouch!" Kato says, feigning pain.

"Let's call Uncle James and tell him!" Kunda says, excited.

I place a video call on my phone. Uncle James answers, his face filling the phone's screen.

"Hello guys! How are you?" Uncle James says.

"We're fine," I say.

"Dad, we have a great idea that we thought you might like," Babirye says, then she explains her idea.

After she is done, Uncle James says nothing for some time.

"What do you think of our idea?" I finally ask. The suspense is killing me.

"Wow!" Uncle James says. "Wow! You guys are geniuses!"

Babirye asks, "So how much shall we earn from the Rainmakers once the government gives you a licence?"

"Now that's a good question, Babirye," Uncle James says. "Can I think about it and get back to you?"

"Sure, she says."

Uncle James ends the call.

I look into Babirye's glistening eyes. She looks so proud of herself that her heart might burst out of her chest. Gosh, she is the most beautiful girl I've ever seen.

"I think I like you," I blurt the words out suddenly, everything else in the room fading away. "Would you like to go out with me for ice cream sometime?"

It's like I have sucked all the air out of the room. I've been rehearsing this moment for weeks, but I hadn't thought it would turn out like this. These weren't the words I'd planned to use.

Damn! I'm stupid!

Kunda and Kato snicker. Sanyu suddenly busies herself on her phone, like nothing has happened.

As for Babirye, her eyes widen like saucers and her jaw drops. Then she covers her open mouth with both her hands.

Time seems still. The three seconds between when I blurt out my nonsense and when she finally says something feel like a gazillion minutes.

I hold my breath.

Please say yes!

"Wait!" Babirye says. "You're kidding, right?"

Then she bursts out into laughter.

Kunda, Kato and Sanyu join her. The tension in the room fades away.

I join in the laughter. But the tension in my chest remains, with a fluttering feeling that I just can't describe.

www.ingramcontent.com/pod-product-compliance
Lightning Source LLC
LaVergne TN
LVHW091717190726
843493LV00001B/343